Les Belles-Soeurs

by **Michel Tremblay**

translated by John Van Burek & Bill Glassco

Talonbooks　　•　　Vancouver　　•　　1991

Copyright © 1972 Leméac Editeur
Translation copyright © 1992 John Van Burek and Bill Glassco

Published with the assistance of the Canada Council.

Talonbooks
P.O. Box 2076, Vancouver, British Columbia, Canada V6B 3S3
www.talonbooks.com

Typeset in Century Oldstyle and printed and bound in Canada by Hignell
Book Printing.

Sixth Revised Printing: August 2003

Canadian Cataloguing in Publication Data

Tremblay, Michel, 1942–
　　　[Belles-soeurs, English]
　　　Les belles soeurs

　　　A play.
　　　Translation of: Les Belles-Soeurs.
　　　ISBN 0-88922-302-5

　　　I. Van Burek, John. II. Glassco, Bill. III. Title.
　　　IV. Title: Belles-soeurs. English
PS8539.R47B413 1992　C842'.54　C92-091066-1
PQ3919.2.T73B413 1992

Les Belles Soeurs was first performed at Théâtre du Rideau-Vert in Montréal, Québec, on August 28, 1968, with the following cast:

GERMAINE LAUZON	Denise Proulx
LINDA LAUZON	Odette Gagnon
ROSE OUIMET	Denise Filiathrault
GABRIELLE JODOIN	Lucille Bélair
LISETTE DE COURVAL	Hélène Loiselle
MARIE-ANGE BROUILLETTE	Marthe Choquette
YVETTE LONGPRÉ	Sylvie Heppel
DES-NEIGES VERRETTE	Denise de Jaguère
THÉRÈSE DUBUC	Germaine Giroux
OLIVINE DUBUC	Nicole LeBlanc
ANGÉLINE SAUVÉ	Anne-Marie Ducharme
RHÉAUNA BIBEAU	Germaine Lemyre
LISE PAQUETTE	Rita Lafontaine
GINETTE MÉNARD	Josée Beauregard
PIERRETTE GUÉRIN	Luce Guilbeault

Directed by André Brassard

Les Belles Soeurs was first performed in English at the St. Lawrence Centre in Toronto, Ontario, on April 3, 1973, with the following cast:

GERMAINE LAUZON	Candy Kane
LINDA LAUZON	Elva-May Hoover
ROSE OUIMET	Monique Mercure
GABRIELLE JODOIN	Araby Lockhart
LISETTE DE COURVAL	Mia Anderson
MARIE-ANGE BROUILLETTE	Deborah Packer
YVETTE LONGPRÉ	Louise Nichol
DES-NEIGES VERRETTE	Maureen Fitzgerald
THÉRÈSE DUBUC	Irene Hogan
OLIVINE DUBUC	Lilian Lewis
ANGÉLINE SAUVÉ	Patricia Hamilton
RHÉAUNA BIBEAU	Nancy Kerr
LISE PAQUETTE	Trudy Young
GINETTE MÉNARD	Suzette Couture
PIERRETTE GUÉRIN	Melanie Morse

Directed by André Brassard

This revised English translation of *Les Belles Soeurs* was first performed at The Stratford Festival in Stratford, Ontario, on June 1, 1991, with the following cast:

GERMAINE LAUZON	Susan Wright
LINDA LAUZON	Shannon Lawson
ROSE OUIMET	Barbara Bryne
GABRIELLE JODOIN	Anne Wright
LISETTE DE COURVAL	Patricia Collins
MARIE-ANGE BROUILLETTE	Michelle Fisk
YVETTE LONGPRÉ	Mary Hitch Blendick
DES-NEIGES VERRETTE	Pat Galloway
THÉRÈSE DUBUC	Nancy Beatty
OLIVINE DUBUC	Sidonie Boll
ANGÉLINE SAUVÉ	Kate Reid
RHÉAUNA BIBEAU	Janet Wright
LISE PAQUETTE	Julia Winder
GINETTE MÉNARD	Ann Baggley
PIERRETTE GUÉRIN	Goldie Semple

Directed by Marti Maraden

- ACT ONE -

LINDA LAUZON enters. She sees four boxes in the middle of the kitchen.

LINDA:
God, what's that? Ma!

GERMAINE:
Is that you, Linda?

LINDA:
Yeah! What are all these boxes in the kitchen?

GERMAINE:
They're my stamps.

LINDA:
Already? Jeez, that was fast.

GERMAINE LAUZON enters.

GERMAINE:
Yeah, it surprised me too. They came this morning right after you left. The doorbell rang. I went to answer it and there's this big fellow standing there. Oh, you'd have liked him, Linda. Just your type. About twenty-two, twenty-three, dark curly hair. Nice little moustache. Real handsome. Anyway, he says to me, "Are you the lady of the house, Mme. Germaine Lauzon?" I said, "yes that's me". And he says, "Good, I've brought your stamps." Linda, I was so excited. I didn't know what to say. Next thing I knew,

5

two guys are bringing in the boxes and the other one's
giving me this speech. Linda, what a talker. And such
manners. I'm sure you would have liked him.

LINDA:
So, what did he say?

GERMAINE:
I can't remember. I was so excited. He told me the
company he works for was real happy I'd won the million
stamps. That I was real lucky, ... Me, I was speechless.
I wish your father had been here, he could have talked to
him. I don't even know if I thanked him.

LINDA:
That's a lot of stamps to glue. Four boxes! One million
stamps, that's no joke!

GERMAINE:
There's only three boxes. The other one's booklets. But I
had an idea, Linda. We're not gonna do all this alone! You
going out tonight?

LINDA:
Yeah, Robert's supposed to call me . . .

GERMAINE:
You can't put it off til tomorrow? Listen, I had an idea. I
phoned my sisters, your father's sister and I went to see
the neighbours. And I've invited them all to come and paste
stamps with us tonight. I'm gonna give a stamp-pasting
party. Isn't that a great idea? I bought some peanuts, and
your little brother went out to get some Coke . . . .

LINDA:
Ma, you know I always go out on Thursdays! It's our night
out. We're gonna go to a show.

GERMAINE:

You can't leave me alone on a night like this. I've got fifteen people coming . . .

LINDA:

Are you crazy! You'll never get fifteen people in this kitchen! And you can't use the rest of the house. The painters are here. Jesus, Ma! Sometimes you're really dumb.

GERMAINE:

Sure, that's right, put me down. Fine, you go out, do just as you like. That's all you ever do anyway. Nothing new. I never have any pleasure. Someone's always got to spoil it for me. Go ahead Linda, you go out tonight, go to your goddamned show. Jesus Christ Almighty, I'm so fed up.

LINDA:

Come on, Ma, be reasonable . . . .

GERMAINE:

I don't want to be reasonable, I don't want to hear about it! I kill myself for you and what do I get in return? Nothing! A big fat nothing! You can't even do me a little favour! I'm warning you, Linda, I'm getting sick of waiting on you, you and everyone else. I'm not your servant, you know. I've got a million stamps to paste and I'm not about to do it myself. Besides, those stamps are for the whole family, which means everybody's gotta do their share. Your father's working tonight but if we don't get done he says he'll help tomorrow. I'm not asking for the moon. Help me for a change, instead of wasting your time with that jerk.

LINDA:

Robert is not a jerk.

GERMAINE:

Sure, he's a genius! Boy, I knew you were stupid, but not

that stupid. When are you going to realize your Robert is a bozo? He doesn't even make sixty bucks a week. All he can do is take you to the local movie house Thursday nights. Take a mother's advice, Linda, keep hanging around with that dope and you'll end up just like him. You want to marry a shoe-gluer and be a strapper all your life?

LINDA:

Shut up, Ma! When you get sore, you don't know what you're saying. Anyway, forget it . . . . I'll stay home . . . Just stop screaming, okay? And by the way, Robert's due for a raise soon and he'll be making lot's more. He's not as dumb as you think. Even the boss told me he might start making big money 'cause they'll put him in charge of something. You wait. Eighty bucks a week is nothing to laugh at. Anyway . . . I'm gonna go phone him and tell him I can't go to the show . . . Hey, why don't I tell him to come and glue stamps with us?

GERMAINE:

Mother of God, I just told you I can't stand him and you want to bring him home tonight. Where the hell are your brains? What did I do to make God in heaven send me such idiots? Just this afternoon, I send your brother to get me a bag of onions and he comes home with a quart of milk. It's unbelievable! You have to repeat everything ten times around here. No wonder I lose my temper. I told you, Linda. The party's for girls. Just girls. Your Robert's not queer, is he?

LINDA:

Okay ma, okay, don't flip your wig. I'll tell him not to come. Jesus, you can't do a thing around here. You think I feel like gluing stamps after working all day.

LINDA starts to dial a number.

Why don't you go dust in the living room, eh? You don't

8

have to listen to what I'm going to say . . . . "Hello, may I
speak to Robert? . . . . When do you expect him? . . . . Okay,
will you tell him Linda phoned? . . . Fine, Mme. Bergeron,
and you? . . . That's good . . . Okay, thanks a lot. Bye."

She hangs up. The phone rings right away.

"Hello?" . . . Ma, it's for you.

GERMAINE: *entering*
Twenty years old and you still can't say "One moment
please" when you answer a phone.

LINDA:
It's only Aunt Rose. Why should I be polite to her?

GERMAINE: *putting her hand over the receiver*
Will you be quiet! What if she heard you?

LINDA:
Who gives a shit?

GERMAINE:
"Hello? Oh, it's you, Rose . . . Yeah, they're here . . . How
'bout that? A million of 'em! They're sitting right in front
of me and I still can't believe it. One million! One million! I
don't know how much that is, but who cares. A million's a
million . . . . Sure, they sent a catalogue. I already had one
but this one's for this year, so it's a lot better. The old one
was falling apart . . . They've got the most beautiful stuff,
wait til you see it. It's unbelievable! I think I'll be able to
take everything they've got. I'll re-furnish the whole
house. I'm gonna get a new stove, new fridge, new kitchen
table and chairs. I think I'll take the red one with the gold
stars. I don't think you've seen that one, ... Oh, it's so
beautiful, Rose. I'm getting new pots, new cutlery, a full
set of dishes, salt and pepper shakers . . . Oh, and you

know those glasses with the "caprice" design. Well, I'm taking a set of those, too. Mme. de Courval got a set last year and she paid a fortune for them, but mine will be free. She'll be mad as hell . . . What? . . . Yeah, she'll be here tonight. They've got those chrome tins for flour and sugar, coffee and stuff . . . . I'm taking it all. I'm getting a Colonial bedroom suite with full accessories. There's curtains, dresser-covers, one of those things you put on the floor beside the bed . . . No, dear, not that . . . New wallpaper . . . Not the floral, Henri can't sleep with flowers . . . I'm telling you Rose, it's gonna be one beautiful bedroom. And the living room! Wait till you hear this . . . . I've got a big TV with a built-in stereo, a synthetic nylon carpet, real paintings . . . You know those Chinese paintings I've always wanted, the ones with the velvet? . . . Aren't they though? Oh, now get a load of this . . . I'm gonna have the same crystal platters as your sister-in-law, Aline! I'm not sure, but I think mine are even nicer. There's ashtrays and lamps . . . I guess that's about it for the living room . . . there's an electric razor for Henri to shave with, shower curtains. So what? We'll put one in. It all comes with the stamps. There's a sunken bathtub, a new sink, bathing suits for everyone . . . No, Rose, I am not too fat. Don't get smart. Now listen, I'm gonna re-do the kid's room, completely. Have you seen what they've got for kids' bedrooms? Rose, it's fabulous! They've got Mickey Mouse all over everything. And for Linda's room . . . Okay, sure, you can just look at the catalogue. But come over right away, the others will be here any minute. I told them to come early. I mean it's gonna take forever to paste all those stamps."

MARIE-ANGE BROUILLETTE enters.

GERMAINE:
"Okay, I've gotta go. Mme. Brouillette's just arrived. Okay, yeah . . . . Yeah . . . Bye!"

10

MARIE-ANGE:
Mme. Lauzon, I just can't help it, I'm jealous.

GERMAINE:
Well, I know what you mean. It's quite an event. But
excuse me for a moment, Mme. Brouillette, I'm not quite
ready. I was talking to my sister, Rose. We can see each
other across the alley, it's handy.

MARIE-ANGE:
Is she gonna be here?

GERMAINE:
You bet! She wouldn't miss this for love nor money. Here,
have a seat and while you're waiting look at the catalogue.
You won't believe all the lovely things they've got. And
I'm getting them all, Mme. Brouillette. The works! The
whole catalogue.

GERMAINE goes into her bedroom.

MARIE-ANGE:
You wouldn't catch me having luck like that. Fat chance.
My life is shit and it always will be. A million stamps! A
whole house. If I didn't bite my tongue, I'd scream.
Typical. The ones with all the luck least deserve it. What
did Mme. Lauzon do to deserve this, eh? Nothing.
Absolutely nothing! She's no better looking than me. In
fact, she's no better period. These contests shouldn't be
allowed. The priest the other day was right. They ought to
be abolished. Why should she win a million stamps and not
me? Why? It's not fair. I work too, I've got kids, too, I
have to wipe their asses, just like her. If anything, my kids
are cleaner than hers. I work like a slave, it's no wonder
I'm all skin and bones. Her, she's fat as a pig. And now,
I'll have to live next door to her and the house she gets for
free. It burns me up, I can't stand it. What's more, there'll

11

be no end to her smart-assed comments 'cause it'll all go straight to her head. She's just the type, the loud-mouthed bitch. We'll be hearing about her goddamned stamps for years. I've a right to be angry. I don't want to die in this shit while madame Fatso here goes swimming in velvet! It's not fair! I'm sick of knocking myself out for nothing! My life is nothing. A big fat zero. And I haven't a cent to my name. I'm fed up. I'm fed up with this stupid, rotten life.

During the monologue, GABRIELLE JODOIN, ROSE OUIMET, YVETTE LONGPRE and LISETTE DE COURVAL have entered. They take their places in the kitchen without paying attention to MARIE-ANGE. The five women get up and turn to the audience.

THE FIVE WOMEN: *together*
This stupid, rotten life! Monday!

LISETTE:
When the sun with his rays starts caressing the little flowers in the fields and the little birdies open wide their little beaks to send forth their little cries to heaven . . .

THE OTHERS:
I get up and I fix breakfast. Toast, coffee, bacon, eggs. I nearly go nuts trying to get the others out of bed. The kids leave for school, my husband goes to work.

MARIE-ANGE:
Not mine, he's unemployed. He stays in bed.

THE FIVE WOMEN:
Then I work. I work like a demon. I don't stop til noon. I wash . . . Dresses, shirts, stockings, sweaters, pants, underpants, bras. The works. I scrub it, wring it out, scrub it again, rinse it . . . My hands are chapped. My back is sore. I curse like hell. At noon, the kids come home. They

eat like pigs, they wreck the house, they leave. In the afternoon I hang out the wash, the biggest pain of all. When
that's finished, I start the supper. They all come home.
They're tired and grumpy. We all fight. But at night, we
watch TV. Tuesday.

LISETTE:
When the sun with his rays . . .

THE OTHERS:
I get up and I fix breakfast. The same goddamn thing.
Toast, coffee, bacon, eggs. I drag the others out of bed
and I shove them out the door. Then it's the ironing. I
work, I work, I work and I work. It's noon before I know
it and the kids are mad because lunch isn't ready. I make
'em baloney sandwiches. I work all afternoon. Suppertime
comes, we all fight. But at night, we watch T.V. Wednesday . . .
Shopping day. I walk all day, I break my back carrying
parcels this big, I come back home exhausted. But I've still
got to make supper. When the others get home I look like
I'm dead. I am. My husband bitches, the kids scream. We
all fight. But at night, we watch T.V. Thursday and Friday . . .
Same thing . . . I work. I slave. I kill myself for my pack
of morons.

THE OTHERS:
Then I spend the day Saturday tripping over the kids and
we all fight. But at night, we watch TV. Sunday we go out,
the whole family, we get on the bus and go for supper with
the mother-in-law. I have to watch the kids like a hawk,
laugh at the old man's jokes, eat the old lady's food, which
everyone says is better than mine . . . At night, we watch
TV. I'm fed up with this stupid, rotten life! This stupid,
rotten life! This stupid, rotten life. This stup . . . .

They sit down suddenly.

13

LISETTE:
On my last trip to Europe . . . .

ROSE:
There she goes with her Europe again. We're in for it now. Once she gets started, there's no shutting her up!

DES-NEIGES VERRETTE comes in. Discreet little greetings are heard.

LISETTE:
I only wished to say that in Europe they don't have stamps. I mean, they have stamps, but not like these ones. Only letter stamping stamps.

DES-NEIGES:
That's no fun! So they don't get presents like us? Sounds pretty dull to me, Europe.

LISETTE:
Oh no, it's very nice despite that . . .

MARIE-ANGE:
Mind you, I've got nothing against stamps, they're useful. If it weren't for the stamps, I'd still be waiting for that thing to grind my meat with. What I don't like is the contests.

LISETTE:
But why? They can make families happy.

MARIE-ANGE:
Maybe, but they're a pain in the ass for the people next door.

LISETTE:
Mme. Brouillette, your language! I speak properly, and I'm none the worse for it.

14

MARIE-ANGE:

I talk the way I talk, and I say what I got to say. I never went to Europe, so I can't afford to talk like you.

ROSE:

Hey, you two, cut it out! We didn't come here to fight. You keep it up, I'm crossing the alley and going home.

GABRIELLE:

What's taking Germaine so long? Germaine!

GERMAINE: *from the bedroom*

Be there in a minute. I'm having a hard time getting into my . . . Well, I'm having a hard time . . . Is Linda there?

GABRIELLE:

Linda! Linda! No, she's not here.

MARIE-ANGE:

I think I saw her go out a while ago.

GERMAINE:

Don't tell me she's snuck out, the little bugger.

GABRIELLE:

Can we start pasting stamps in the meantime?

GERMAINE:

No wait! I'm going to tell you what to do. Don't start yet, wait till I get there. Chat for a bit.

GABRIELLE:

"Chat for a bit?" What are we going to chat about . . .

The telephone rings.

ROSE:

My God, that scared me! "Hello . . . No, she's out, but if you want to wait I think she'll be back in a few minutes."

She puts the receiver down, goes out on the balcony and shouts.

"Linda! Linda, telephone!"

LISETTE:

So, Mme. Longpré how does marriage agree with your daughter Claudette?

YVETTE:

Oh, she loves it. She's having a ball. She told me about her honeymoon, you know.

GABRIELLE:

Where did they go to?

YVETTE:

Well, he won a trip to the Canary Islands, eh? So you see, they had to put the wedding ahead a bit . . . .

ROSE: *laughing*

The Canary Islands! A honeymoon in bird shit, eh?

GABRIELLE:

Come on, Rose!

ROSE:

What?

DES-NEIGES:

The Canary Islands, where's that?

LISETTE:

We stopped by there, my husband and I, on our last trip to Europe. It's a real . . . It's a very pleasant country. The women only wear skirts.

ROSE:

The perfect place for my husband!

LISETTE:

And I'm afraid the natives are not very clean. Of course, in Europe, people don't wash.

DES-NEIGES:

It shows, too. Look at those Italians next door to me. You wouldn't believe how that woman stinks.

They all burst out laughing.

LISETTE: *insinuating*

Did you ever notice her clothesline, on Monday?

DES-NEIGES:

No, why?

LISETTE:

Well, all I know is this . . . . Those people don't have any underwear.

MARIE-ANGE:

You're kidding!

ROSE:

I don't believe it!

YVETTE:

You gotta be joking!

17

LISETTE:

It's the God's truth! Take a look for yourselves next Monday. You'll see.

YVETTE:

No wonder they stink.

MARIE-ANGE:

Maybe she's too modest to hang them outside.

The others laugh.

LISETTE:

Modest! A European? They don't know what it means. Just look at their movies you see on TV. It's appalling. They stand right in the middle of the street and kiss. On the mouth, too! It's in their blood, you know. Take a look at that Italian's daughter when she brings her friends around . . . . Her boyfriends, that is . . . It's disgusting what she does, that girl. She has no shame! Which reminds me, Mme. Ouimet. I saw your Michel the other day . . .

ROSE:

Not with that slut, I hope!

LISETTE:

I'm afraid so.

ROSE:

You must be mistaken. It couldn't have been him.

LISETTE:

I beg your pardon, but the Italians are my neighbours, too. The two of them were on the front balcony . . . I suppose they thought no one could see them . . .

DES-NEIGES:
    It's true, Mme. Ouimet, I saw them myself. I tell you,
    they were necking like crazy.

ROSE:
    The little bastard! As if one pig in the family's not enough.
    By pig I mean my husband. Can't even watch a girl on
    TV without getting a . . . . Without getting worked up.
    Goddamn sex! They never get enough, those Ouimets.
    They're all alike, they . . .

GABRIELLE:
    Rose, you don't have to tell the whole world . . .

LISETTE:
    But we're very concerned . . .

DES-NEIGES and MARIE-ANGE:
    Yes, we are . . .

YVETTE:
    To get back to my daughter's honeymoon . . .

GERMAINE: *entering*
    Here I am, girls!

    Greetings, "how are you's", etc.

    So, what have you all been talking about?

ROSE:
    Oh, Mme. Longpré was telling us about her daughter
    Claudette's honeymoon . . . .

GERMAINE:
    Really? *To YVETTE* Hello, dear . . . *To ROSE* And
    what was she saying?

ROSE:
Sounds like they had a great trip. They met all these
people. They went on a boat. They were visiting islands,
of course, The Canary Islands . . . They went fishing and
they caught fish this big. They ran into some couples they
knew . . . . Old friends of Claudette's. Then they came
back together and, oh yes, they stopped over in New
York. Mme. Longpré was giving us all the details . . .

YVETTE:
Well . . .

ROSE:
Eh, Mme. Longpré, isn't that right?

YVETTE:
Well, as a matter of fact . . .

GERMAINE:
You tell your daughter, Mme Longpré that I wish her all
the best. Of course, we weren't invited to the wedding,
but we wish her well anyway.

There is an embarrassed silence.

GABRIELLE:
Hey! It's almost seven! The rosary!

GERMAINE:
Dear God, my novena for Ste.-Thérèse. I'll get Linda's radio.

She goes out.

ROSE:
What does she want with Ste.-Thérèse, especially after
winning all that?

DES-NEIGES:
Maybe she's having trouble with her kids . . . .

GABRIELLE:
No, she would have told me . . . .

GERMAINE: *from the bedroom*
Goddamn it! Where did she put that frigging radio?

ROSE:
I don't know, Gaby. Our sister usually keeps things
to herself.

GABRIELLE:
Not with me. She tells me everything. You, you're such a
blabbermouth . . . .

ROSE:
You've got a lot of nerve! What do you mean, blabbermouth?
Gabrielle Jodoin! My mouth's no bigger than yours.

GABRIELLE:
Come off it, you know you can't keep a secret!

ROSE:
Well, I never . . . If you think . . .

LISETTE:
Wasn't it you, Mme. Ouimet, who just said we didn't
come here to quarrel?

ROSE:
Hey, you mind your own business. Besides, I didn't say
"quarrel." I said "fight".

GERMAINE comes back in with a radio.

GERMAINE:
What's going on? I can hear you at the other end of the house!

GABRIELLE:
Nothing, it's our sister again . . .

GERMAINE:
Settle down, Rose. You're supposed to be the life of the party . . .
No fighting tonight.

ROSE:
You see! In our family we say "fight".

> *GERMAINE turns on the radio. We hear a voice saying the rosary. All the women get down on their knees. After a few "Hail Marys" a great racket is heard outside. The women scream and run to the door.*

GERMAINE:
Oh my God! My sister-in-law Thérèse's mother-in-law just fell down three flights of stairs!

ROSE:
Did you hurt yourself, Mme. Dubuc?

GABRIELLE:
Rose, shut up! She's probably dead!

THERESE: *from a distance*
Are you all right, Mme. Dubuc? *A faint moan is heard.* Wait a minute. Let me get the wheelchair off you. Is that better? Now I'm gonna help you get back in your chair. Come on, Mme. Dubuc, make a little effort. Don't be so limp! Ouch!

DES-NEIGES:

Here, Mme. Dubuc. Let me give you a hand.

THERESE:

Thanks Mlle. Verrette. You're so kind.

The other women come back into the room.

ROSE:

Germaine, shut off the radio. I'm a nervous wreck!

GERMAINE:

What about my novena?

ROSE:

How far have you gotten?

GERMAINE:

I'm only up to seven, but I promised to do nine.

ROSE:

So, pick it up tomorrow and you'll be finished on Saturday.

GERMAINE:

It's not for nine days, it's for nine weeks.

THERESE DUBUC and DES-NEIGES VERRETTE enter with OLIVINE DUBUC, who is in a wheelchair.

My God, she wasn't hurt bad, I hope.

THERESE:

No, no, she's used to it. She falls out of her chair ten times a day. Whew! I'm all out of breath. It's no joke, hauling this thing up three flights of stairs. You got something to drink, Germaine?

GERMAINE:

Gaby, give Thérèse a glass of water.

She approaches OLIVINE DUBUC.

And how are you today, Mme. Dubuc?

THERESE:

Don't get too close, Germaine. She's been biting lately.

In fact, OLIVINE DUBUC tries to bite GERMAINE's hand.

GERMAINE:

My god, you're right! She's dangerous! How long has she been doing that?

THERESE:

Shut off the radio, Germaine, it's getting on my nerves. I'm too upset after what's happened.

GERMAINE reluctantly shuts off the radio.

GERMAINE:

It's alright, Thérèse, I understand.

THERESE:

Honestly, you don't know what it's like, I'm at the end of my tether! You can't imagine my life since I got stuck with my mother-in-law. It's not that I don't love here, the poor woman, I pity her. But she's sick, and so temperamental. I've gotta watch her like a hawk!

DES-NEIGES:

How come she's out of the hospital?

THERESE:

Well, you see, Mlle. Verrette, three months ago my husband got a raise, so welfare stopped paying for his mother. If she'd stayed there, we would have had to pay all the bills ourselves.

MARIE-ANGE:

My, my, my . . .

YVETTE:

That's awful.

DES-NEIGES:

Dreadful!

During THERESE's speech, GERMAINE opens the boxes and distributes the stamps and books.

THERESE:

We had to bring her home. It's some cross to bear, believe me! Don't forget, that woman's ninety-three years old. It's like having a baby in the house. I have to dress her, undress her, wash her . . . .

DES-NEIGES:

God forbid!

YVETTE:

You poor thing.

THERESE:

No, it's no fun. Why only this morning, I said to Paul . . . he's my youngest . . . "Maman's going shopping, so you stay here and take good care of Granny." Well, when I got home, Mme Dubuc had dumped a quart of molasses all over herself and was playing in it like a kid. Of course, Paul was nowhere to be seen. I had to clean the table, the floor, the wheelchair . . .

25

GERMAINE:
What about Mme. Dubuc?

THERESE:
I left her like that for the rest of the afternoon. That'll teach her. If she's gonna act like a baby, I'll treat her like one. Do you realize I have to spoon feed her?

GERMAINE:
My poor Thérèse. How I feel for you.

DES-NEIGES:
You're too good, Thérèse.

GABRIELLE:
Much too good, I agree.

THERESE:
What can you do, we all have our crosses to bear.

MARIE-ANGE:
If you ask me, Thérèse, you've got a heavy one!

THERESE:
Oh well, I don't complain. I just tell myself that our Lord is good and He's gonna help me get through.

LISETTE:
I can't bear it, it makes me want to weep.

THERESE:
Now, Mme. de Courval, don't overdo it.

DES-NEIGES:
All I can say Mme. Dubuc, is you're a real saint.

GERMAINE:

Well, now that you've got stamps and booklets, I'll put a little water in some saucers and we can get started, eh? We don't want to spend the night yacking.

She fills a few saucers and passes them around. The women start pasting stamps in the books. GERMAINE goes out on the balcony.

GERMAINE:

If Linda were here, she could help me! Linda! Linda! Richard, have you seen Linda? I don't believe it! She's got the nerve to sit and drink Coke while I'm slaving away! Be an angel, will you, and tell her to come home right away? Come see Mme. Lauzon tomorrow and she'll give you some peanuts and candy, if there's any left, okay? Go on, Sweetie, and tell her to get home this minute!

She comes back inside.

The little bitch. She promised to stay home.

MARIE-ANGE:

Kids are all the same.

THERESE:

You can say that again! They got no respect.

GABRIELLE:

You're telling me. At our house, it's unbearable. Ever since my Raymond started his *cours classique* he's changed something awful . . . We don't recognize him! He walks around with his nose in the air like he's too good for us. He speaks Latin, at the table! We have to listen to his awful music. Can you imagine, classical music in the middle of the afternoon? And when we don't want to watch his stupid TV concerts, he throws a fit. If there's one thing I hate it's classical music.

ROSE:
Ah! You're not the only one.

THERESE:
I agree. It drives me crazy. Clink! Clank! Bing, Bang, Bong!

GABRIELLE:
Of course, Raymond says we don't understand it. As if there's something to understand! Just because he's learning all sorts of nonsense at school, he thinks he can treat us like dirt. I've got half a mind to yank him out and put him to work.

ALL THE WOMEN:
Kids are so ungrateful! Kids are so ungrateful!

GERMAINE:
Be sure to fill those books, eh, girls? Stamps on every page.

ROSE:
Relax, Germaine, you'd think we'd never done it before.

YVETTE:
Isn't it getting a little warm in here? Maybe we could open the window a bit . . .

GERMAINE:
No, no, not with the stamps. It'll make a draft.

ROSE:
Come on, Germaine, they're not birds. They won't fly away. Oh, speaking of birds, last Sunday I went to see Bernard, my oldest. Well, you've never seen so many birds in one house. The house is one big bird cage. And it's her doing, you know. She's nuts about birds! And she doesn't want to kill any. Too soft-hearted, but surely to God there's a limit. Listen to this, it's a scream.

Spotlight on ROSE OUIMET.

ROSE:

I'm telling you the woman's nuts. I joke about it but
really, it's not funny. Anyway, last Easter, Bernard
picked up this bird cage for the two kids. Some guy at the
tavern needed money, so he sold it to him cheap . . . .
Well, the minute he got it in the house, she went
bananas. Fell head over heels in love with his birds. No
kidding. She took better care of them than she did her
kids. Of course, in no time at all the females were laying
eggs . . . And when they started to hatch, Manon thought
they were so cute. She didn't have the heart to get rid of
them. You've got to be crazy, eh? So she kept them! The
whole flock! God knows how many she's got. I never
tired to count 'em . . . But, believe me, every time I set
foot in the place I nearly go out of my mind! But wait,
you haven't heard anything yet. Every day around two,
she opens up the cage and out come her stupid birds.
What happens? They fly all over the house. They shit all
over everything, including us, and we run after them
cleaning it all up. Of course, when it's time to get them
back in the cage, they don't want to go. They're having
too much fun! So Manon starts screaming at the kids,
"Catch Maman's little birdies, Maman's too tired". So
the kids go charging after the birds and the place is a
frigging circus. Me, I get the hell out! I go sit on the
balcony and wait till they've all been caught.

The women laugh.

And those kids! God, what brats! Oh, I like them okay,
they're my grandchildren. But Jesus, do they drive me
nuts. Our kids weren't like that. Say what you like. Young
people today, they don't know how to bring up their kids.

GERMAINE:
You said it!

YVETTE:
That's for sure.

ROSE:
I mean, take the bathroom. Now we wouldn't have let
our kids play in there. Well, you should have seen it on
Sunday. The kids went in there like they were just going
about their business and in no time flat they'd turned the
place upside down. I didn't say a word! Manon always says
I talk too much. But I could hear them alright and they
were getting on my nerves. You know what they were
doing? They took the toilet paper, and they unrolled the
whole goddamn thing. Manon just yelled "Look, you kids,
Maman's gonna get angry." A lot of good that did. They
didn't pay any attention. They kept right on going. I would've
skinned 'em alive, the little buggers. And were they having
a ball! Bruno, the youngest . . . Can you imagine calling a
kid "Bruno?" . . . Anyway, Bruno climbed into the
bathtub fully dressed and all rolled up in toilet paper and
turned on the water. Listen, he was laughing so hard he
nearly drowned! He was making boats out of soggy paper
and the water was running all over the place. A real flood!
Well, I had to do something. I mean, enough is enough,
so I gave them a licking and sent them off to bed.

YVETTE:
That's exactly what they needed!

ROSE:
Their mother raised a stink, of course, but I'll be damned
if I was gonna let them carry on like that. Manon, the
dim-wit, she just sits there peeling potatoes and listening
to the radio. Oh, she's a winner, that one! But I guess
she's happy. The only thing she worries about is her

birds. Poor Bernard! At times I really feel sorry for him, being married to that. He should have stayed home with me. He was a lot better off . . .

She burst out laughing.

YVETTE:
Isn't she a riot! There's no stopping her.

GABRIELLE:
Yeah, there's never a dull moment with Rose.

ROSE:
I always say, when it's time to laugh, might as well have a good one. Every story has a funny side, you know? Even the sad ones . . . .

THERESE:
You're damn lucky if you can say that, Mme. Ouimet. It's not everyone . . .

DES-NEIGES:
We understand, dear. It must be hard for you to laugh with all your troubles. You're far too good, Mme. Dubuc! You're always thinking of others . . .

ROSE:
That's right, you should think of yourself sometimes. You never go out.

THERESE:
I don't have time! When would you have me go out? I have to take care of her . . . Ah! If only that was all . . .

GERMAINE:
Thérèse, don't tell me there's more.

THERESE:

If you only knew! Now that my husband's making some money the family thinks we're millionaires. Why only yesterday, a sister-in-law of my sister-in-law's came to the door with her hand out. Well, you know me. When she told me her story it just broke my heart. So I gave here some old clothes I didn't need anymore . . . Ah, she was so happy . . . . weeping with gratitude . . . she even kissed my hands.

DES-NEIGES:

I'm not surprised. You deserve it!

MARIE-ANGE:

Mme. Dubuc, I really admire you.

THERESE:

Oh, don't say that . . . .

DES-NEIGES:

No, no, no. You deserve it.

LISETTE:

You certainly do, Mme. Dubuc. You deserve our admiration and I assure you, I shan't forget you in my prayers.

THERESE:

Well, I always say, "If God put poor people on this earth, they gotta be encouraged."

GERMAINE:

When you're through filling your books there, instead of piling them on the table, why don't we put them back in the box? . . . Rose, give me a hand. We'll take out the empty books and put in the full ones.

ROSE:

Good idea. My God! Look at all these books. We gotta fill
all them tonight?

GERMAINE:

Sure, why not? Besides, everyone's not here yet,
so we . . .

DES-NEIGES:

Who else is coming, Mme. Lauzon?

GERMAINE:

Rhéauna Bibeau and Angeline Sauvé are supposed to
come by after the funeral parlour. One of Mlle. Bibeau's
old girlfriends has a daughter whose husband died. His
name was . . . Baril, I think . . .

YVETTE:

Not Rosaire Baril.

GERMAINE:

Yeah, I think that's it . . .

YVETTE:

But I knew him well! I used to go out with him for Godsake.
How do you like that! I'd have been a widow today.

GABRIELLE:

Guess what, girls? I got the eight mistakes in last Saturday's
paper. It's the first time I ever got'em all and I've been
trying for six months . . . I sent in the answer . . .

YVETTE:

Did you win anything yet?

GABRIELLE:

Do I look like someone who's ever won anything?

THERESE:
Hey, Germaine, what are you going to do with all
these stamps?

GERMAINE:
Didn't I tell you? I'm going to re-decorate the whole
house. Wait a minute . . . Where did I put the catalogue? . . .
Ah, here it is. Look at that, Thérèse. I'm gonna have all
that for nothing.

THERESE:
For nothing! You mean it's not going to cost you
a cent?

GERMAINE:
Not a cent! Aren't these contests wonderful?

LISETTE:
That's not what Mme. Brouillette said a while ago . . .

GERMAINE:
What do you mean?

MARIE-ANGE:
Mme. de Courval, really!

ROSE:
Well, come on, Mme. Brouillette. Don't be afraid to say
what you think. You said earlier you don't like these
contests because only one family wins.

MARIE-ANGE:
Well, it's true! All these lotteries and contests are unfair.
I'm against them.

GERMAINE:
Just because you never won anything.

MARIE-ANGE:
Maybe, maybe, but they're still not fair.

GERMAINE:
Not fair, my eye! You're jealous, that's all. You said so yourself the minute you walked in. Well, I don't like jealous people, Mme. Brouillette. I don't like them one bit! In fact, if you really want to know, I can't stand them!

MARIE-ANGE:
Well! In that case, I'm leaving!

GERMAINE:
No, no don't go! Look I'm sorry . . . I'm all nerves tonight, I don't know what I'm saying. We'll just forget it, okay? You have every right to your opinions. Every right. Just sit back down and keep pasting.

ROSE:
Our sister's, afraid of losing one of her workers.

GABRIELLE:
Shut up, Rose! You're always sticking your nose where it don't belong.

ROSE:
What's eating you? I can't even open my mouth?

MARIE-ANGE:
Alright, I'll stay. But I still don't like them.

From this point on, MARIE-ANGE BROUILLETTE will steal all the books she fills. The others will see what she's doing right from the start, except for GERMAINE, obviously, and they will decide to follow suit.

LISETTE:

Well, I figured out the mystery charade in last month's Chatelaine. It was very easy . . . My first syllable is a Persian king . . .

ROSE:

Onassis?

LISETTE:

No, a *Persian* king . . . It's a "shah" . . .

ROSE:

That's a Persian?

LISETTE:

Why, of course . . .

ROSE: *laughing*

That's his tough luck!

LISETTE:

My second is for killing bugs . . . No one? . . . Oh, well, "Raid" . . . .

ROSE:

My husband's a worm, do you think it would work on him? . . . She's really nuts with all this stuff, eh?

LISETTE:

And the whole thing is a social game . . .

ROSE:

Spin the bottle!

GABRIELLE:

Rose, will you shut up for Godsake! *to LISETTE* Scrabble?

LISETTE:
Oh, come now, it's simple . . . Shah-raid . . . Charade!

YVETTE:
Ah . . . What's a charade?

LISETTE:
Of course, I figured it out in no time . . . It was so easy . . .

YVETTE:
So, did you win anything?

LISETTE:
Oh, I didn't bother to send it in. I just did it for the challenge . . . Besides, do I look like I need to win things?

ROSE:
Well, I like mystery words, hidden words, crosswords, turned-around words, bilingual words. All that stuff with words. It's my specialty. I'm a champ, you know, I've broken all the records! Never miss a contest . . . Costs me two bucks a week just for stamps!

YVETTE:
So did you win yet?

ROSE: *looking at GERMAINE*
Do I look like somebody who's ever won anything?

THERESE:
Mme. Dubuc, will you let go of my saucer? . . . There, now you've done it! You've spilled it! That's the last straw!

She socks her mother-in-law on the head and the latter settles down a little.

GABRIELLE:
Wow! You don't fool around! Aren't you afraid you'll hurt her?

THERESE:
No, no. She's used to it. It's the only way to shut her up. My husband figured it out. If you give her a good bash on the head, it seems to knock her out a while. That way she stays in her corner and we get some peace.

Blackout.

Spotlight on YVETTE LONGPRE.

YVETTE:
When my daughter Claudette got back from her honeymoon, she gave me the top part of her wedding cake. I was so proud! It's such a lovely piece. A miniature sanctuary all made of icing. It's got a red velvet stairway leading up to a platform and on top of the platform stand the bride and groom. Two little dolls all dressed up like newly-weds. There's even a priest to bless them and behind him there's an altar. It's all icing. I've never seen anything so beautiful. Of course, we paid a lot for the cake. After all, six levels! It wasn't all cake though. That would have cost a fortune. Just the first two levels were cake. The rest was wood. But it's amazing, eh? You'd never have guessed. Anyway, when my daughter gave me the top part, she had it put under this glass bell. It looked so pretty, but I was afraid it would spoil . . . you know, without air. So I took my husband's glass knife . . . He's got a special knife for cutting glass . . . And I cut a hole in the top of the bell. Now the air will stay fresh and the cake won't go bad.

DES-NEIGES:
Me too. I took a stab at a contest a few weeks ago. You had to find a slogan for some bookstore . . . I think it was

Hachette or something . . . Anyway, I gave it a try . . . I came up with "Hachette will chop the cost of your books." Not bad, eh?

YVETTE:
Yeah, but did you win anything?

DES-NEIGES:
Do I look like somebody who's ever won anything?

GERMAINE:
By the way, Rose, I saw you cutting your grass this morning. You should buy a lawn-mower.

ROSE:
What for? I get along fine with scissors. Besides it keeps me in shape.

GERMAINE:
You were puffing away like a steam engine.

ROSE:
I'm telling you, it's good for me. Anyway, I can't afford a lawn-mower. Even if I could, that's the last thing I'd buy.

GERMAINE:
I'll be getting a lawn-mower with my stamps . . .

DES-NEIGES:
Her and her stamps, she's starting to get on my nerves!

She hides a booklet in her purse.

ROSE:
What are you gonna do with a lawn-mower on the third floor?

GERMAINE:

You never know, it might come in handy. And who knows, we might move someday.

DES-NEIGES:

I suppose she's going to tell us she needs a new house for all the stuff she's gonna get with her lovely stamps.

GERMAINE:

You know, we probably will need a bigger place for all the stuff I'm gonna get with my stamps.

DES-NEIGES VERRETTE, MARIE-ANGE BROUILLETTE and THERESE DUBUC all hide two or three books each.

Rose, if you want, you can borrow my lawn-mower.

ROSE:

No way! I might bust it. I'd be collecting stamps for the next two years just to pay you back.

The women laugh.

GERMAINE:

Don't be smart.

MARIE-ANGE:

Isn't she something! Can you beat that!

THERESE:

Hey, I forgot to tell you. I guessed the mystery voice on the radio . . . It was Duplessis . . . My husband figured it out 'cause it was an old voice. I sent in twenty-five letters just to be sure they'd get it. And for extra luck, I signed my youngest boy's name, Paul Dubuc . . . .

YVETTE:
Did you win anything yet?

THERESE: *looking to GERMAINE*
Do I look like someone who's ever won anything?

GABRIELLE:
Say, do you know what my husband's gonna get me for
my birthday?

ROSE:
Same as last year. Two pairs of nylons.

GABRIELLE:
No sir-ee! A fur coat. Of course, it's not real fur, but
who cares? I don't think real fur's worth buying anymore.
The synthetics they make nowadays are just as nice. In
fact, sometimes nicer.

LISETTE:
Oh, I disagree . . .

ROSE:
Sure, we all know who's got a fat mink stole!

LISETTE:
Well, if you ask me, there's no substitute for authentic,
genuine fur. Incidentally, I'll be getting a new stole in the
autumn. The one I have now is three years old and it's
starting to look . . . . Well, a bit ratty. Mind you, it's still
mink, but . . . .

ROSE:
Shut your mouth, you bloody liar! We know goddamn well
your husband's up to his ass in debt because of your mink
stoles and trips to Europe! She's got no more money than
the rest of us and she thinks her farts smell like perfume!

41

LISETTE:

Mme. Jodoin, if your husband wants to buy my stole, I'll sell it to him cheap. Then you'll have real mink. After all, between friends . . . .

YVETTE:

You know the inflated objects game in the paper, the one where you're supposed to guess what the objects are? Well, I guessed them. There was a screw, a screw-driver and some kind of bent up hook.

THE OTHERS:

So . . .

YVETTE sits down.

GERMAINE:

You know Daniel, Mme. Robitaille's little boy? He fell off the second floor balcony the other day. Not even a scratch! How 'bout that?

MARIE-ANGE:

Don't forget he landed on Mme. Turgeon's hammock. And Monsieur Turgeon was in it at the time . . .

GERMAINE:

That's right. He's in hospital for three months.

DES-NEIGES:

Speaking of accidents, I heard a joke the other day . . .

ROSE:

Well, aren't you gonna tell us?

DES-NEIGES:

Oh, I couldn't. It's too racy . . .

ROSE:

Come on, Mlle. Verrette! We know you've got a stack of them . . .

DES-NEIGES:

No. I'm too embarrassed. I don't know why, but I am . . . .

GABRIELLE:

Don't be such a tease, Mlle. Verrette. You know darn well you're gonna tell us anyway . . .

DES-NEIGES:

Well . . . Alright . . . There was this nun who got raped in an alley . . .

ROSE:

Sounds good!

DES-NEIGES:

And the next morning they found her lying in the yard, a real mess, her habit pulled over her head, moaning away . . . so this reporter comes running over and he says to her, "Excuse me, Sister, but could you tell us something about this terrible thing that's happened to you?" Well, she opens her eyes, looks up at him and in a very small voice she says, "Again, please".

All the women burst out laughing except for LISETTE DE COURVAL who appears scandalized.

ROSE:

Christ Almighty, that's hysterical! I haven't heard such a good one for ages. I'm gonna pee my pants! Mlle. Verrette, where in the world do you get them?

GABRIELLE:

You know where, from her travelling salesman . . .

43

DES-NEIGES:
   Mme. Jodoin, please!

ROSE:
   That's right too. Her travelling salesman . . .

LISETTE:
   I don't understand.

GABRIELLE:
   Mme. Verrette has a travelling salesman who comes to
   sell her brushes every month. I think she likes him more
   than his brushes.

DES-NEIGES:
   Mme. Jodoin, honestly!

ROSE:
   One thing's for sure, Mlle. Verrette has more brushes
   than anyone in the parish. Hey, I saw your boyfriend the
   other day . . . He was sitting in the restaurant . . . He
   must have been to see you, eh?

DES-NEIGES:
   Yes, he was—but I assure you, there's nothing between us.

ROSE:
   That's what they all say.

DES NEIGES:
   Really, Mme. Ouimet, you're always twisting things to
   make people look bad. Monsieur Simard is a very nice
   man.

ROSE:
   Yeah, but who's to say you're a nice lady? Now, now,
   Mlle. Verrette, don't get angry. I'm only pulling your leg.

DES-NEIGES:

Then don't say things like that. Of course, I'm a nice
lady, a thoroughly respectable one, too. By the way, the
last time he was over, Henri . . . 'Er . . . Monsieur
Simard was telling me about a project he has in mind . . .
And he asked me to extend you all an invitation. He
wants me to organize a demonstration next week . . . At
my house. He chose me because he knows my house . . .
It'd be for a week Sunday, right after the rosary. I need
at least ten people if I'm gonna get my gift . . . You know,
they give away those fancy cups to the one who holds the
demonstration . . . Fantasy Chinaware . . . You should see
them, they're gorgeous. They're souvenirs he brought
back from Niagara Falls . . . They must have cost a fortune.

ROSE:

You bet, we'll go, eh, girls? I love demonstrations! Any
door prizes?

DES-NEIGES:

I don't know. I suppose. Maybe . . .Anyway, I'll provide
snacks . . .

ROSE:

That's more than you get around here. We'll be lucky to
see a glass of water!

OLIVINE DUBUC tries to bite her daughter-in-law.

THERESE:

Mme. Dubuc, if you don't stop that I'm gonna lock you in
the bathroom and you can stay there for the rest of the evening.

Blackout. Spotlight on DES-NEIGES VERRETTE.

DES-NEIGES:

The first time I saw him I thought he was ugly . . . it's

45

true. He's not good-looking. When I opened the door he took off his hat and said, "Would you be interested in buying some brushes, Madame?" I slammed the door in his face. I never let a man in the house! Who knows what might happen . . . . The only one who gets in is the paper boy. He's still too young to get any wrong ideas. Well, a month later my friend with the brushes came back. There was a terrible snowstorm outside, so I let him stand in the hall. Once he was in the house, I was frightened, but I told myself he didn't look dangerous, even if he wasn't good looking . . . He's always well-dressed . . . Not a hair out of place . . . He's a real gentleman . . . . And so polite! Well, he sold me a couple of brushes and then he showed me his catalogue.
There was one that I wanted, but he didn't have it with him, so he said I could place an order. Ever since then, he's come back once a month. Sometimes I don't buy a thing. He just comes in and we chat for a while. He's such a nice man. When he speaks, you forget he's ugly. And he knows so many interesting things! The man must travel all over the province! I think . . . . I think I'm in love with him . . . I know it's crazy. I only see him once a month, but it's so nice when we're together. I'm so happy when he comes. I've never felt this way before. Never. Men never paid much attention to me. I've always been . . . unattached. But he tells me about his trips, and all kinds of stories . . . Sometimes they're a bit risqué, but honestly, they're so funny! I must admit, I've always liked stories that are a bit off-colour . . . And it's good for you to tell them sometimes. Not all his jokes are dirty, mind you. Lots of them are clean. And it's only lately that he's been telling me the spicy ones. Sometimes they're so dirty I blush! The last time he came he took my hand when I blushed. I nearly went out of my mind. My insides went all funny when he put his big hand on mine. I need him so badly! I don't want him to go away! Sometimes, just sometimes, I dream about him. I dream . . . that we're married. I need

him to come and see me. He's the first man that ever cared about me. I don't want to lose him! I don't want to! If he goes away, I'll be all alone again, and I need . . . someone to love . . .

She lowers her eyes and murmurs.

I need a man.

The lights come on again. LINDA LAUZON, GINETTE MENARD and LISE PAQUETTE enter.

GERMAINE:
Ah, there you are!

LINDA:
I was at the restaurant.

GERMAINE:
I know you were are the restaurant. You keep hanging around there, you're gonna end up like your Aunt Pierrette . . . In a whore house.

LINDA:
Lay off, Ma! You're making a stink over nothing.

GERMAINE:
I asked you to stay home . . .

LINDA:
Look, I went to get cigarettes and I ran into Lise and Ginette . . .

GERMAINE:
That's no excuse. You knew I was having company, why didn't you come right home. You do it on purpose, Linda. You do it just to make my blood boil. You want me to

47

blow my stack in front of my friends? Is that it? You want
me to swear in public? Well, Jesus Christ Almighty,
you've succeeded! But don't think you're off the hook
yet, Linda Lauzon. I'll take care of you later.

ROSE:
This is no time to bawl her out, Germaine!

GABRIELLE:
Rose, you mind your own business.

LINDA:
So, I'm a little late, my God, it's not the end of the world!

LISE:
It's our fault, Mme. Lauzon.

GINETTE:
Yeah, it's our fault.

GERMAINE:
I know it's your fault. And I've told Linda a hundred
times not to run around with tramps. But you think she
gives a damn? Sometimes I'd like to strangle her!

ROSE:
Now, Germaine . . .

GABRIELLE:
Rose, I told you, stay out of this! You got that? It's their
business. It's nothing to do with you.

ROSE:
Hey, get off my back! What's with you anyway? Linda's
getting bawled out and she hasn't done a goddamn thing!

GABRIELLE:
It's none of our business!

48

LINDA:

Leave her alone, Aunt Gaby. She's only trying to defend me.

GABRIELLE:

Don't you tell me what to do! I'm your Godmother!

GERMAINE:

You see what she's like! Day in and day out! I never brought her up to act this way.

ROSE:

Now that you mention it, how do you bring up your kids?

GERMAINE:

Hah! You should talk! . . . . Your kids . . .

LINDA:

Go on, Aunt Rose, tell her. You're the only one who can give it to her good.

GERMAINE:

So, you're siding with your Aunt Rose now are you? You've forgotten what you said when she phoned a while ago, eh? You've forgotten about that? Come on, Linda, tell Aunt Rose what you said about her.

LINDA:

That was different . . .

ROSE:

Why, what did she say?

GERMAINE:

Well, she answered the phone when you called, right? And she was too rude to say, "One moment, please," so I told her to be more polite with you . . . .

LINDA:

Will you shut up, Ma! That has nothing to do with it.

ROSE:

I want to know what you said, Linda.

LINDA:

It's not important, I was mad at her.

GERMAINE:

She said, "It's only Aunt Rose. Why should I be polite to her?"

ROSE:

I don't believe it . . . You said that?

LINDA:

I told you, I was mad at her!

ROSE:

I never thought that of you, Linda. There, you've let me down. You've really let me down.

GABRIELLE:

Let them fight it out themselves, Rose.

ROSE:

You bet I'll let 'em fight. Go on, Germaine. Knock her silly, the little brat! You wanna know something, Linda? Your mother's right. If you're not careful, you'll end up like your Aunt Pierrette. I've got a good mind to slap your face!

GERMAINE:

Just you try it! You don't lay a hand on my kids! If they need a beating, I'll do it. Nobody else!

THERESE:

Will you please stop bickering, I'm tired!

DES-NEIGES:

Lord, yes, you're wearing us out.

THERESE:

You'll wake up my mother-in-law and get her going again.

GERMAINE:

She's your problem, not mine! Why didn't you leave her at home?

THERESE:

Germaine Lauzon!

GABRIELLE:

Well, she's right. You don't go out to parties with a ninety-three year old cripple.

LISETTE:

Mme. Jodoin, didn't I just hear you tell your sister to mind her own business?

GABRIELLE:

Keep your big nose out of this, you stuck up bitch! Shut your yap and keep pasting or I'll shut it for you.

LISETTE DE COURVAL gets up.

LISETTE:

Gabrielle Jodoin!

OLIVINE DUBUC spills the saucer she has been playing with.

THERESE:

Mme Dubuc, for Godsake!

GERMAINE:

Aw, shit, my tablecloth!

ROSE:
She's soaked me, the old bag!

THERESE:
That's not true! You weren't even close!

ROSE:
Sure, call me a liar right to my face!

THERESE:
Rose Ouimet, you are a liar!

GERMAINE:
Look out, she's falling out of her chair!

DES-NEIGES:
Oh, no, she's on the floor, again!

THERESE:
Somebody give me a hand.

ROSE:
Not me, no way!

GABRIELLE:
Pick her up yourself.

DES-NEIGES:
Here, I'll help you, Mme. Dubuc.

THERESE:
Thank you, Mlle. Verrette.

GERMAINE:
And you, Linda, you watch your step for the rest of the evening.

LINDA:
I feel like going back to the restaurant.

GERMAINE:
Do that and you won't set foot in this house again, you hear?

LINDA:
Sure, I've heard it a thousand times.

LISE:
Can it, Linda . . .

THERESE:
For Godsake, Mme. Dubuc, make a little effort. You go limp like that on purpose.

MARIE-ANGE:
I'll hold the chair.

THERESE:
Thank you . . . .

ROSE:
If it was me, I'd take that lousy chair and . . .

GABRIELLE:
Rose, don't start again!

THERESE:
Whew! What I go through . . . .

GABRIELLE:
Hey, will you get a load of de Courval, still pasting her stamps . . . The bloody snob. As if nothing had happened! I guess we're not good enough for her.

Blackout.

Spotlight on LISETTE DE COURVAL.

LISETTE:
It's like living in a barnyard. Leopold told me not to come and he was right. I should have stayed home. We don't belong with these people. Once you've tasted life on an ocean liner and have to return to this, well . . . . It's enough to make you weep . . . I can still see myself, stretched out on the deck chair, a Book-of-the-Month in my lap . . . And that lieutenant who was giving me the eye . . . My husband says he wasn't, but he didn't see what I saw . . . Mmmmm . . . . That was some man. Maybe I should have encouraged him a little more . . . *She sighs.* . . . And Europe! Everyone there is so refined! So much more polite than here. You'd never meet a Germaine Lauzon in Europe. Never! Only people of substance. In Paris, you know, everyone speaks so beautifully and there they talk real French . . . Not like here . . . I despise everyone of them. I'll never set foot in this place again! Léopold was right about these people. These people are cheap. We shouldn't mix with them. Shouldn't talk about them . . . They should be hidden away somewhere. They don't know how to live! We broke away from this and we must never, ever go back. Dear God, they make me so ashamed!

The lights come back up.

LINDA:
I've had it. I'm leaving . . .

GERMAINE:
The hell you are! I'm warning you Linda! . . .

LINDA:
"I'm warning you, Linda!" Is that all you know how to say?

LISE:
Linda, don't be stupid.

GINETTE:
Let's stay.

LINDA:
No, I'm leaving. I've listened to enough crap for one night.

GERMAINE:
Linda, I forbid you to leave!

VOICE OF A NEIGHBOUR:
Will you stop screaming up there. We can't hear ourselves think!

ROSE goes out on the balcony.

ROSE:
Hey, you! Get back in your house.

NEIGHBOUR:
I wasn't talking to you!

ROSE:
Oh yes, you were. I'm just as loud as the rest of them!

GABRIELLE:
Rose, get in here!

DES-NEIGES: *referring to the neighbour*
Don't pay any attention to her.

NEIGHBOUR:
I'm gonna call the cops!

ROSE:
Go right ahead, we need some men up here.

GERMAINE:
Rose Ouimet, get back in this house! And you, Linda . . .

LINDA:
I'm leaving. See ya!

She goes out with GINETTE and LISE.

GERMAINE:
She's gone! Gone! Walked right out! I don't believe it! That kid will be the death of me. I'm gonna smash something. I'm gonna smash something!

ROSE:
Germaine, control yourself.

GERMAINE:
Making a fool of me in front of everyone! *She starts sobbing.* My own daughter . . . I'm so ashamed!

GABRIELLE:
Come on, Germaine. It's not that bad . . .

LINDA'S VOICE:
Hey, if it isn't Mlle. Sauvé. How are you doing?

ANGELINE'S VOICE:
Hello, sweetheart, how are you?

ROSE:
Germaine, they're here. Blow your nose and stop crying.

LINDA'S VOICE:
Not bad, thanks.

RHEAUNA'S VOICE:
Where are you off to?

LINDA'S VOICE:
I was gonna go to the restaurant, but now that you're here, I think I'll stay.

LINDA, GINETTE and LISE enter with ANGELINE and RHEAUNA.

ANGELINE:
Hello, everybody.

RHEAUNA:
Hello.

THE OTHERS:
Hello, hello. Come on in, how have you been . . . *etc.*

RHEAUNA:
What an awful climb, Mme. Lauzon. I'm all out of breath.

GERMAINE:
Well, have a seat . . .

ROSE:
You're out of breath? Don't worry, my sister's getting an elevator with her stamps.

They all laugh except RHEAUNA and ANGELINE who don't understand.

GERMAINE:
Very funny, Rose! Linda, go get some more chairs . . .

LINDA:
Where? There aren't any more.

GERMAINE:
Go ask Mme. Bergeron if she'll lend us some . . .

LINDA: *to the girls*
Come on, guys . . .

GERMAINE: *low to LINDA*
We make peace for now, but wait til the others
have gone . . .

LINDA:
I'm not scared of you. If I came back it's because Mlle.
Sauvé and Mlle. Bibeau showed up, not because of you.

LINDA goes out with her friends.

DES-NEIGES:
Here, take my seat, Mlle. Bibeau . . .

THERESE:
Yes, come and sit next to me . . .

MARIE-ANGE:
Sit down here, Mlle. Bibeau . . .

ANGELINE and RHEAUNA:
Thank you. Thanks very much.

RHEAUNA:
I see you're pasting stamps.

GERMAINE:
We sure are. A million of 'em!

RHEAUNA:
Dear God, a million! How are you getting on?

ROSE:

Not bad . . . But my tongue's paralyzed.

RHEAUNA:

You've been doing it with your tongue?

GABRIELLE:

Of course not, she's just being smart.

ROSE:

Good old Bibeau. Sharp as a tack!

ANGELINE:

Why don't we give you a hand?

ROSE:

Okay. As long as you don't give us some tongue!

She bursts out laughing.

GABRIELLE:

Rose, don't be vulgar!

GERMAINE:

So, how was the funeral parlour?

Black out. Spotlight on ANGELINE and RHEAUNA.

RHEAUNA:

I tell you, it came as a shock . . .

ANGELINE:

But I thought you hardly knew him.

RHEAUNA:

I knew his mother. So did you. Remember, we went to
school together. I watched that man grow up . . .

ANGELINE:

Such a shame. Gone, just like that. And us, we're still here.

RHEAUNA:

Ah, but not for long . . .

ANGELINE:

Rhéauna, please . . .

RHEAUNA:

I know what I'm talking about. You can tell when the end is near. I've suffered. I know.

ANGELINE:

Ah, when it comes to that, we've both had our share. I've suffered, too.

RHEAUNA:

I've suffered a lot more than you, Angeline. Seventeen operations! A lung, a kidney, one of my breasts . . . Gone! I'm telling you, there's not much left.

ANGELINE:

And me with my arthritis that won't let up. But Mme . . . What was her name . . . You know, the wife of the deceased . . . She gave me a recipe . . . She says it works wonders.

RHEAUNA:

But you've tried everything. The doctors have all told you, there's nothing you can do. There's no cure for arthritis.

ANGELINE:

Doctors, doctors! . . . I've had it with doctors. All they think about is money. They bleed you to death and go to California for the winter. You know, Rhéauna, the doctor said he'd get well, Monsieur . . . What was his name again? The one who died?

RHEAUNA:

Monsieur Baril . . .

ANGELINE:

That's it. I can never remember it. It's easy enough, too.
Anyhow, the doctor told Monsieur Baril that he had nothing
to worry about . . . And look what happened . . . Only
forty years old . . .

RHEAUNA:

Forty years old! That's young to die.

ANGELINE:

He sure went fast . . .

RHEAUNA:

She told me how it happened. It's so sad . . .

ANGELINE:

Really? I wasn't there. How did it happen?

RHEAUNA:

When he got home from work on Monday night, she
thought he was looking a bit strange. He was white as a
sheet, so she asked him how he felt. He said he felt okay
and they started supper . . . Well, now, the kids were
making a fuss at the table and Monsieur Baril got mad and
had to punish Rolande. That's his daughter . . . of course,
after that, he looked like he was ready to drop . . . she
didn't take her eyes off him for a second . . . But she
told me later that it happened so fast she didn't have time
to do a thing. All of a sudden he said he felt funny and
over he went . . . His face right in the soup. That was it!

ANGELINE:

Lord, have mercy. So sudden! I tell you, Rhéauna, it's
frightening. It gives me the shivers.

RHEAUNA:

Isn't it the truth? We never know when God's going to come for us. He said it Himself, "I'll come like a thief."

ANGELINE:

Don't talk like that, it scares me. I don't want to die that way. I want to die in my bed . . . have time to make my confession . . . .

RHEAUNA:

Oh, God forbid that I should die before confessing! Angéline, promise me you'll call the priest the minute I'm feeling weak. Promise me that.

ANGELINE:

You know I will. You've asked me a hundred times. Didn't I get him there for your last attack? You had Communion and everything.

RHEAUNA:

I'm so afraid to die without the last rites.

ANGELINE:

But what do you have to confess, Rhéauna?

RHEAUNA:

Don't say that, Angéline. Don't ever say that! We're never too old to sin.

ANGELINE:

If you ask me, Rhéauna, you'll go straight to heaven. You've got nothing to worry about. Hey! Did you notice Baril's daughter? The way she's changed! She looks like a corpse.

RHEAUNA:

Isn't it the truth. Poor Rolande. She's telling everyone that she killed her father. Its because of her that he got

62

mad, you see, at supper . . . Oh I feel so sorry for
her . . . And her mother. What a tragedy! Such a loss for
everyone. They'll miss him so . . . .

ANGELINE:
You're telling me . . . The father. Mind you, it's not as
bad as the mother, but still . . .

RHEAUNA:
True. Losing the mother is worse. You can't replace
a mother.

ANGELINE:
Did you see how nice he looked? . . . Like a young man.
He was even smiling . . . . I could have sworn he was
asleep. But I still think he's better off where he is . . .
You know what they say, it's the ones who stay behind
who most deserve the pity. Him, he's fine now . . . Ah, I
still can't get over how good he looked. Almost like he
was breathing.

RHEAUNA:
Yeah! But he wasn't.

ANGELINE:
But I can't imagine why they put him in that suit . . .

RHEAUNA:
What do you mean?

ANGELINE:
Didn't you notice? He was wearing a blue suit. You don't
do that when you're dead. A blue suit is much too light.
Now, navy-blue would be okay, but powder blue . . .
Never! When you're dead, you wear a black suit.

RHEAUNA:

Maybe he didn't have one. They're not that well off, you know.

ANGELINE:

Dear God, you can rent a black suit! And look at Mme. Baril's sister! In green! At a funeral parlour! And did you notice how much she's aged? She looks years older than her sister . . .

RHEAUNA:

She is older.

ANGELINE:

Don't be silly, Rhéauna, she's younger.

RHEAUNA:

No, she isn't.

ANGELINE:

Why sure, Rhéauna, listen! Mme Baril is at least thirty-seven, but her sister . . .

RHEAUNA:

She's well over forty!

ANGELINE:

Rhéauna, she isn't!

RHEAUNA:

She's at least forty-five . . .

ANGELINE:

That's what I'm telling you. She's aged so much, she looks a lot older than she is . . . Listen, my sister-in-law, Rose-Aimée, is thirty-six and the two of them went to school together . . . .

RHEAUNA:

Well, anyway, it doesn't surprise me she's aged so
fast . . . What with the life she leads . . .

ANGELINE:

I'm not sure they're true, all those stories.

RHEAUNA:

They must be! Mme. Baril tries to hide it 'cause it's her
sister . . . But the truth always comes out. It's like Mme.
Lauzon and her sister, Pierrette. Now, if there's one
person I can't stand, it's Pierrette Guérin. A shameless
hussy! Nothing but shame to her whole family. I tell you,
Angéline, I wouldn't want to see her soul. It must be
black as coal.

ANGELINE:

You know, Rhéauna, deep down inside, Pierrette isn't all bad.

Spotlight on GERMAINE LAUZON.

GERMAINE:

My sister, Pierrette, I've had nothing to do with her for a
long time. Not after what she did. When she was young,
she was so good, and so pretty. But now, she's nothing
but a whore. My sisters and I were nuts about her. We
spoiled her rotten. And look what it got us . . . I don't
understand. I don't understand. Papa used to call her his
pepper pot. He was so crazy about his little Pierrette.
When he'd put her on his knee, you could tell he was
happy. And the rest of us weren't even jealous . . .

ROSE:

We'd say, "She's the youngest. It's always that way, it's
the youngest who gets the attention." When she started
school, we dressed her like a princess. I was already
married, but I remember as if it were yesterday. Oh, she

was so pretty! Like Shirley Temple! And so quick at school. A lot better than me, that's for sure. I was lousy at school . . . I was the class clown, that's all I was ever good for . . . But her, the little bugger, always coming home with prizes. First in French, first in Arithmetic, first in Religion . . . Yeah, Religion! She was pious as a nun, that kid. I tell you, the Sisters were nuts about her! But to see her today . . . . I almost feel sorry for her. She must need help sometimes . . . She must get so lonely . . . .

GABRIELLE:
When she finished school, we asked her what she wanted to do. She wanted to be a teacher. She was all set to begin her training . . . . And then she met her Johnny.

THE THREE SISTERS:
Goddamn Johnny! He's a devil out of hell! It's all his fault she turned out the way she did. Goddamn Johnny! Goddamn Johnny!

RHEAUNA:
What do you mean, not all bad! You've got to be pretty low to do what she did. Do you know what Mme. Longpré told me about her?

ANGELINE:
No, what?

THERESE:
Ow!!!

The lights come back up. THERESE DUBUC gives her mother-in-law a sock on the head.

GERMAINE:
Beat her brains out, if you have to Thérèse but do something!

THERESE:

Sure, beat her brains out! Look, I'm doing all I can to keep her quiet. I'm not about to kill her just to make you happy.

ROSE:

If it was up to me, I'd shove her off the balcony . . .

THERESE:

What? Say that again, Rose. I didn't hear you!

ROSE:

I was talking to myself.

THERESE:

You're scared, eh?

ROSE:

Me, scared?

THERESE:

Yes, Rose. Scared!

MARIE-ANGE:

Don't tell me there's gonna be another fight.

ANGELINE:

Has there been a fight?

RHEAUNA:

Oh, who was fighting?

ANGELINE:

We should have come sooner.

THERESE:

I won't stand for that. She insulted my mother-in-law! My husband's mother!

LISETTE:
There they go again!

ROSE:
She's so old! She's useless!

GERMAINE:
Rose!

GABRIELLE:
Rose, that's cruel! Aren't you ashamed?

THERESE:
Rose Ouimet, I'll never forgive you for those words! Never!

ROSE:
Ah, piss off!

ANGELINE:
Who had a fight?

ROSE:
You want to know everything, eh, Mademoiselle Sauvé?
You want all the gory details?

ANGELINE:
Mme. Ouimet!

ROSE:
So you can blab it all over town, eh? Isn't that it?

RHEAUNA:
Rose Ouimet, I don't lose my temper often, but I will not
allow you to insult my friend.

MARIE-ANGE: *to herself*
I'll just grab a few more while no one's looking.

GABRIELLE: *who has seen her*
What are you doing there, Mme. Brouillette?

ROSE:
Fine, I've said enough. I'll shut up.

MARIE-ANGE:
Shhhh! Take these and keep quiet!

LINDA, GINETTE and LISE arrive with the chairs.
There is a great hullabalou. All the women change
places, taking advantage of the occasion to steal more stamps.

Don't be afraid, take them!

DES-NEIGES:
Aren't you overdoing it?

THERESE:
Hide these in your pocket, Mme. Dubuc, . . . No! Damn
it! Hide them!

GERMAINE:
You know that guy who runs the meat shop, what a thief!

The door opens suddenly and PIERRETTE GUERIN
comes in.

PIERRETTE:
Hi, everybody!

THE OTHERS:
Pierrette!

LINDA:
Great! It's Aunt Pierrette!

ANGELINE:

Oh my God, Pierrette!

GERMAINE:

What are you doing here? I told you I never wanted to see you again.

PIERRETTE:

I heard that my big sister, Germaine, had won a million stamps, so I decided to come over and have a look. *She sees ANGELINE* Well, I'll be goddamned! Angéline! What are you doing here?

Everyone looks at ANGELINE.

Blackout.

- ACT TWO -

The second act begins with PIERRETTE's entrance.
Hence the last six lines of Act One are repeated now. The
door opens suddenly and PIERRETTE GUERIN comes in.

PIERRETTE:
Hi, everybody!

THE OTHERS:
Pierrette!

LINDA:
Great! It's Aunt Pierrette!

ANGELINE:
Oh, my God, Pierrette!

GERMAINE:
What are you doing here? I told you I never wanted to see
you again.

PIERRETTE:
I heard that my big sister, Germaine, had won a million
stamps, so I decided to come over and have a look. *She*
sees ANGELINE Well, I'll be goddamned! Angéline!
What are you doing here?

Everyone looks at ANGELINE.

71

ANGELINE:
My God! I'm caught.

GERMAINE:
What do you mean, Angéline?

GABRIELLE:
How come you're talking to Mlle. Sauvé?

ROSE:
You oughtta be ashamed!

PIERRETTE:
Why? We're real good friends, eh, Géline?

ANGELINE:
Oh! I think I'm going to faint!

ANGELINE pretends to faint.

RHEAUNA:
Good heavens, Angéline!

ROSE:
She's dead!

RHEAUNA:
What?

GABRIELLE:
Don't be ridiculous! Rose, you're getting carried away again.

PIERRETTE:
She hasn't even fainted. She only pretending.

PIERRETTE approaches ANGELINE.

GERMAINE:
Don't you touch her!

PIERRETTE:
Mind your own business! She's my friend.

RHEAUNA:
What do you mean, your friend?

GERMAINE:
Don't try to tell us Mlle. Sauvé is a friend of yours!

PIERRETTE:
Of course she is! She comes to see me at the club almost every Friday night.

ALL THE WOMEN:
What!

RHEAUNA:
That's impossible.

PIERRETTE:
Ask her! Hey, Géline, isn't it true what I'm saying? Come on, stop playing dead and answer me. Angéline, we all know you're faking! Tell them. Isn't it true you come to the club?

ANGELINE: *after a silence*
Yes, it's true.

RHEAUNA:
Oh, Angéline! Angéline!

SOME OF THE WOMEN:
Dear God, this is dreadful!

SOME OTHER WOMEN:
   Dear God, this is horrible!

LINDA, GINETTE and LISE:
   Holy shit, that's great!

   The lights go out.

RHEAUNA:
   Angéline! Angéline!

   Spotlight on ANGELINE and RHEAUNA.

ANGELINE:
   Rhéauna, you must understand . . .

RHEAUNA:
   Don't you touch me! Get away!

THE WOMEN:
   Who would have thought . . . Such a horrible thing!

RHEAUNA:
   I'd never have thought this of you. You, in a club. And
   every Friday night! It's not possible. It can't be true.

ANGELINE:
   I don't do anything wrong, Rhéauna. All I have is a Coke.

THE WOMEN:
   In a club! In a night club!

GERMAINE:
   God only knows what she does there.

ROSE:
   Maybe she tries to get picked up.

ANGELINE:
But I tell you, I don't do anything wrong!

PIERRETTE:
It's true. She doesn't do anything wrong.

ROSE, GERMAINE, and GABRIELLE:
Shut up, you demon. Shut up!

RHEAUNA:
You're no longer my friend, Angéline. I don't know you.

ANGELINE:
Listen to me, Rhéauna, you must listen! I'll explain everything and then you'll see!

ROSE, GERMAINE and GABRIELLE:
A club! the fastest road to hell!

ALL THE WOMEN: *except the girls*
The road to hell, the road to hell! If you go there, you'll lose your soul! Cursed drink, cursed dancing! That's the place where our men go wrong and spend their money on women of sin!

ROSE, GERMAINE and GABRIELLE:
Women of sin like you, Pierrette!

ALL THE WOMEN: *except the girls*
Shame on you, Angéline Sauvé, to spend your time in this sinful way!

RHEAUNA:
But Angéline, a club! It's worse than hell!

PIERRETTE: *laughing heartily*
If hell's anything like the club I work in, I wouldn't mind eternity there!

ROSE, GERMAINE and GABRIELLE:
Shut up, Pierrette. The devil has your tongue!

LINDA, GINETTE and LISE:
The devil? Come on! Get with the times! The clubs are not the end of the world! They're no worse than any place else. They're fun! They're lots of fun. The clubs are lots of fun.

THE WOMEN:
Ah! Youth is blind! Youth is blind! You're gonna lose yourselves and then you'll come crying to us. But it'll be too late! It'll be too late! Watch out! You be careful of these cursed places! We don't always know when we fall, but when we get back up, it's too late!

LISE:
Too late! It's too late! Oh my God, it's too late!

GERMAINE:
I hope at least you'll go to confession, Angéline Sauvé!

ROSE:
And to think that every Sunday I see you at Communion . . . Communion with a sin like that on your conscience!

GABRIELLE:
A mortal sin!

ROSE, GERMAINE and GABRIELLE:
How many times have we been told . . . It's a mortal sin to set foot in a club!

ANGELINE:
That's enough. Shut up and listen to me!

THE WOMEN:
Never! You've no excuse!

ANGELINE:
Rhéauna, will you listen to me! We're old friends. We've been together for thirty-five years. You mean a lot to me, but there are times when I want to see other people. You know how I am. I like to have fun. I grew up in church basements and I want to see other things. Clubs aren't all bad, you know. I've been going for four years and I never did anything wrong. And the people who work there, they're no worse than us. I want to meet people, Rhéauna! Rhéauna, I've never laughed in my life!

RHEAUNA:
There are better places to laugh. Angéline, you're going to lose your soul. Tell me you won't go back.

ANGELINE:
Listen, Rhéauna, I can't! I like to go there, don't you understand. I like it!

RHEAUNA:
You must promise or I'll never speak to you again. It's up to you. It's me or the club. If you only knew how much that hurts, my best friend sneaking off to a night club. How do you think that looks, Angéline? What will people say when they see you going there? Especially where Pierrette works. It's the lowest of them all! You must never go back, Angéline, you hear? If you do, it's finished between us. Finished! You ought to be ashamed!

ANGELINE:
Rhéauna, you can't ask me not to go back . . . Rhéauna, answer me!

RHEAUNA:
Until you promise, not another word!

The lights come up. ANGELINE sits in a corner.
PIERRETTE joins her.

ANGELINE:
Why did you have to come here tonight?

PIERRETTE:
Let them talk. They love to get hysterical. They know
damn well you don't do anything wrong at the club. In
five minutes, they'll forget all about it.

ANGELINE:
You think so, eh? Well, what about Rhéauna? You think
she'll forgive me just like that? And Mme. de Courval
who's in charge of recreation for the parish, also
President of the Altar Society at Our Lady of Perpetual
Help! You think she'll continue speaking to me? And your
sisters who can't stand you because you work in a club!
I'm telling you it's hopeless! Hopeless!

GERMAINE:
Pierrette!

PIERRETTE:
Listen, Germaine, Angéline feels bad enough. So let's not
fight, eh? I came here to see you and paste stamps and I
want to stay. And I don't have the plague, okay? Just
leave us alone. Don't worry. The two of us'll stay out of
your way. After tonight, if you want, I'll never come back
again. But I can't leave Angeline alone.

ANGELINE:
You can leave if you want, Pierrette . . .

PIERRETTE:
No, I want to stay.

ANGELINE:
Okay, then I'll go.

LISETTE:
Why don't they both leave!

ANGELINE gets up.

ANGELINE: *To RHEAUNA*
Are you coming?

RHEAUNA doesn't answer.

Okay. I'll leave the door unlocked . . .

She goes towards the door. The lights go out. Spotlight on ANGELINE SAUVE.

It's easy to judge people. It's easy to judge them, but you have to look at both side of the coin. The people I've met in that club are my best friends. No one has ever treated me so well . . . Not even Rhéauna. I have fun with those people. I can laugh with them. I was brought up by nuns in the parish halls who did the best they could, poor souls, but knew nothing. I was fifty-five years old when I learned to laugh. And it was only by chance. Because Pierrette took me to her club one night. Oh, I didn't want to go. She had to drag me there. But, you know, the minute I got in the door, I knew what it was to go through life without having any fun. I suppose clubs aren't for everyone, but me, I like them. And of course, it's not true that I only have a Coke. Of course, I drink liquor! I don't have much, but still, it makes me happy. I don't do anyone any harm and I buy myself two hours of pleasure every week. But this was bound to happen someday. I knew I'd get caught sooner or later. I knew it. What am I going to do now? Dear God, what am I going to do? *Pause.* Damn it all! Everyone deserves to get some fun out of life! *Pause.* I always said that if I got caught I'd stop going . . . But I don't know if I can . . . And Rhéauna will never go along with that. *Pause.* Ah, well, I suppose Rhéauna is worth more than Pierrette. *She gives a long sigh.* I guess the party's over . . . .

She goes off. Lights out. Spotlight on YVETTE LONGPRE.

YVETTE:
Last week, my sister-in-law, Fleur-Ange, had a birthday. They had a real nice party for her. There was a whole gang of us there. First there was her and her family, eh? Oscar David, her husband, Fleur-Ange David, that's her, and their seven kids: Raymonde, Claude, Lisette, Fernand, Réal, Micheline and Yves. Her husband's parents, Aurèle David and his wife, Ozéa David, were there too. Next, there was my sister-in-law's mother, Blanche Tremblay. Her father wasn't there 'cause he's dead . . . Then there were the other guests: Antonio Fournier, his wife Rita, Germaine Gervais, also, Wilfred Gervais, Armand Campeau, Daniel Lemoyne and his wife, Rose-Aimée, Roger Joly, Hormidas Guay, Simmone Laflamme, Napoléon Gauvin, Anne-Marie Turgeon, Conrad Joanette, Léa Liasse, Jeanette Landreville, Nona Laplante, Robertine Portelance, Gilbert Morrissette, Lilianne Beaupré, Virginie Latour, Alexandre Thibodeau, Ovila Gariépy, Roméo Bacon and his wife Juliette, Mimi Bleau, Pit Cadieux, Ludger Champagne, Rosaire Rouleau, Roger Chabot, Antonio Simard, Alexandrine Smith, Philemon Langlois, Eliane Meunier, Marcel Morel, Grégoire Cinq-Mars, Théodore Fortier, Hermine Héroux and us, my husband, Euclide, and me. And I think that's just about everyone . . . .

The lights come back up.

GERMAINE:
Okay, now let's get back to work, eh?

ROSE:
On your toes, girls. Here we go!

DES-NEIGES:
We're not doing badly, are we? Look at all I've pasted . . .

MARIE-ANGE:
What about all you've stolen . . .

LISETTE:
You want to hand me some more stamps, Mme. Lauzon.

GERMAINE:
Sure . . . coming right up . . . Here's a whole bunch.

RHEAUNA:
Angeline! Angeline! It can't be true!

LINDA: *To PIERRETTE*
Hi, Aunt Pierrette.

PIERRETTE:
Hi! How're you doing?

LINDA:
Oh, not too hot. Ma and I are always fighting and I'm really getting sick of it. She's always bitching about nothing, you know? I'd sure like to get out of here.

GERMAINE:
The retreats will be starting pretty soon, eh?

ROSE:
Yeah! That's what they said last Sunday.

MARIE-ANGE:
I hope we won't be getting the same priest as last year . . . .

GERMAINE:
Me too! I didn't like him either. What a bore.

PIERRETTE:
Well, what's stopping you? You could come and stay with me . . . .

LINDA:
Are you kidding? They'd disown me on the spot!

LISETTE:
No, we've got a new one coming this year.

DES-NEIGES:
Oh yeah? Who's it gonna be?

LISETTE:
A certain Abbé Rochon. They say he's excellent. I was talking to l'Abbé Gagné the other day and he tells me he's one of his best friends . . . .

ROSE: *To GABRIELLE*
There she goes again with her l'Abbé Gagné. We'll be hearing about him all night! You'd think she was in love with him. L'Abbé Gagné this, l'AbbéGagné that. Well, if you want my opinion, I don't like l'Abbé Gagné.

GABRIELLE:
I agree. He's too modern for me. It's okay to take care of parish activities, but he shouldn't forget he's a priest! A man of God!

LISETTE:
Oh, but the man is a saint . . . You should get to know

him, Mme. Dubuc. I'm sure you'd like him . . . When he speaks, you'd swear it was the Lord himself talking to us.

THERESE:
Don't overdo it . . .

LISETTE:
And the children! They adore him. Oh, that reminds me, the children in the parish are organizing a variety night for next month. I hope you can all make it because it should be very impressive. They've been practicing for ages . . .

DES-NEIGES:
What's on the programme?

LISETTE:
Well, it's going to be very good. There'll be all sorts of things. Mme. Gladu's little boy is going to sing . . .

ROSE:
Again! I'm getting sick of that kid. Besides, since he went on television, his mother's got her nose in the air. She thinks she's a real star!

LISETTE:
But the child has a lovely voice.

ROSE:
Oh yeah? Well, he looks like a girl with his mouth all puckered up like a turkey's ass.

GABRIELLE:
Rose!

LISETTE:
Diane Aubin will give a demonstration of aquatic swimming . . . We'll be holding the event next door to the city pool, it will be wonderful . . .

ROSE:
Any door prizes?

LISETTE:
Oh yes, lots. And the final event of the evening will be a giant bingo.

THE OTHER WOMEN: *except the girls*
A bingo!

Blackout.

When the lights come back up, the women are all at the edge of the stage.

LISETTE:
Ode to Bingo!

While ROSE, GERMAINE, GABRIELLE, THERESE and MARIE-ANGE recite the Ode to Bingo, the four other women call out bingo numbers in counterpoint.

ROSE, GERMAINE, GABRIELLE, THERESE and MARIE-ANGE:
Me, there's nothing in the world I like more than bingo. Almost every month we have one in the parish. I get ready two days ahead of time; I'm all wound up, I can't sit still, it's all I can think of. And when the big day arrives, I'm so excited, housework's out of the question. The minute supper's over, I get all dressed up, and a team of wild horses couldn't hold me back. I love playing bingo! I adore playing bingo! There's nothing in the world can beat bingo! When we arrive at the apartment where we're going to play we take off our coats and head straight for the tables. Sometimes it's the living room the lady's cleared, sometimes it's the kitchen. Sometimes it's even the bedroom. We sit at the tables, distribute the cards, set up the chips and the game begins!

The women who are calling the numbers continue alone for a moment.

I'm so excited, I go bananas. I get all mixed up, I sweat like a pig, screw up the numbers, put my chips in the wrong squares, make the caller repeat the numbers, I'm in an awful state! I love playing bingo! I adore playing bingo! There's nothing in the world can beat bingo! The game's almost over. I've got three more tries. Two down and one across. I'm missing the B14! I need the B14! I want the B14! I look at the others. Shit, they're as close as I am. What am I gonna do? I've gotta win! I've gotta win! I've gotta win!

LISETTE:
   B14!

THE OTHERS:
   Bingo! Bingo! I've won! I knew it! I knew I couldn't lose! I've won! Hey, what did I win?

LISETTE:
   Last month we had Chinese dog door stops. But this month, this month, we've got ashtray floor lamps!

THE OTHERS:
   I love playing bingo! I adore playing bingo! There's nothing in the world beats bingo! What a shame they don't have 'em more often. The more they have, the happier it makes me! Long live the Chinese dogs! Long live the ashtray floor lamps! Long live bingo!

   Lights to normal.

ROSE:
   I'm getting thirsty.

GERMAINE:
   Oh, God, I forgot the drinks! Linda, get out the Cokes.

OLIVINE:
Coke . . . Coke . . . Yeah . . . Yeah, Coke . . .

THERESE:
Relax, Mme. Dubuc. You'll get your Coke like everyone else. But drink it properly! No spilling it like last time.

ROSE:
She's driving me up the wall with her mother-in-law . . .

GABRIELLE:
Forget it, Rose. There's been enough fighting already.

GERMAINE:
Yeah! Just keep quiet and paste. You're not doing a thing!

Spotlight on the refrigerator. The following scene takes place by the refrigerator door.

LISE: *to LINDA*
I've got to talk to you, Linda . . .

LINDA:
I know, you told me at the restaurant . . . But it's hardly a good time . . .

LISE:
It won't take long and I've got to tell somebody, I can't hide it much longer. I'm too upset. And Linda, you're my best friend . . . Linda, I'm going to have a baby.

LINDA:
What! But that's crazy! Are you sure?

LISE:
Yes, I'm sure. The doctors told me.

LINDA:
What are you gonna do?

LISE:

I don't know. I'm so depressed! I haven't told my
parents yet. My father'll kill me, I know he will. When
the doctor told me, I felt like jumping off the balcony . . .

PIERRETTE:

Listen, Lise . . .

LINDA:

You heard?

PIERRETTE:

Yeah! I know you're in a jam, kid, but . . . I might be
able to help you . . .

LISE:

Yeah? How?

PIERRETTE:

Well, I know a doctor . . .

LINDA:

Pierrette, she can't do that!

PIERRETTE:

Come on, it's not dangerous . . . He does it twice a
week, this guy.

LISE:

I've thought about it already, Linda . . . But I didn't know
anyone . . . And I'm scared to try it alone.

PIERRETTE:

Don't ever do that! It's too dangerous! But with this
doctor . . . I can arrange it, if you like. A week from now
you'll be all fixed up.

LINDA:

Lise, you can't do that!

LISE:

What else can I do? It's the only way out. I don't want
the thing to be born. Look what happened to Manon
Belair. She was in the same boat and now her life's all
screwed up because she's got that kid on her hands.

LINDA:

What about the father? Can't he marry you?

LISE:

Are you kidding! I don't even know where he is. He just
took off somewhere. Sure, he promised me the moon. We
were gonna be happy. He was raking it in, I thought
everything was roses. One present after another. No end
to it. It was great while it lasted . . . but Goddamn it, this
had to happen. It just had to. Why is it always me who
ends up in the shit? All I ever wanted was a proper life
for myself. I'm sick of working at Kresges. I want to
make something of myself, you know, I want to be
somebody. I want a car, a decent place to live, nice
clothes. My uniforms for the restaurant are all I own, for
Chrissake. I never have any money, I always have to
scrounge, but I want that to change. I don't want to be
cheap anymore. I came into this world by the back door,
but by Christ I'll go out by the front! Nothing's gonna
stop me. Nothing. You watch, Linda, you'll see I was right.
Give me two or three years and you'll see that Lise Paquette
is a somebody. And money, she's gonna have it, okay?

LINDA:

You're off to a bad start.

LISE:

That's just it! I've made a mistake and I want to correct

it. After this I'll start fresh. You understand, don't you, Pierrette?

PIERRETTE:
Sure, I do. I know what it is to want to be rich. Look at me. When I was your age, I left home because I wanted to make some money. But I didn't start by working in a dime store. Oh, no! I went straight to the club. Because that's where the money was. And it won't be long now before I hit the jackpot. Johnny's promised me . . .

ROSE, GERMAINE and GABRIELLE:
Goddamn Johnny! Goddamn Johnny!

GINETTE:
What's going on over here?

LISE:
Nothing, nothing. *To PIERRETTE.* We'll talk about it later . . .

GINETTE:
Talk about what?

LISE:
Forget it. It's nothing!

GINETTE:
Can't you tell me?

LISE:
Look, will you leave me alone?

PIERRETTE:
Come on, we can talk over here . . .

GERMAINE:
What's happening to those Cokes?

LINDA:
Coming, coming . . . .

The lights come back up.

GABRIELLE:
Hey, Rose, you know that blue suit of yours? How much did you pay for it?

ROSE:
Which one?

GABRIELLE:
You know, the one with the white lace around the collar?

ROSE:
Oh, that one . . . I got it for $9.98.

GABRIELLE:
That's what I thought. Imagine, today I saw the same one at Reitmans for $14.98.

ROSE:
No kidding! I told you I got it cheap, eh?

GABRIELLE:
I don't know how you do it. You always find the bargains.

LISETTE:
My daughter Micheline just found a new job. She's started to work with those F.B.I. machines.

MARIE-ANGE:
Oh yeah! I hear those things are tough on the nerves.

The girls who work them have to change jobs every six months. My sister-in-law, Simonne's daughter, had a nervous breakdown over one. Simonne just called today to tell me about it.

ROSE:
Oh my God, I forgot, Linda, you're wanted on the phone!

Linda runs to the phone.

LINDA:
"Hello? Robert? How long have you been waiting?"

GINETTE:
Tell me.

LISE:
No. Beat it, will you? I want to talk to Pierrette . . . Go on, get lost!

GINETTE:
Okay, I get the message! You're happy to have me around when there's nobody else, eh? but when someone more interesting comes along . . .

LINDA:
"Listen, Robert, how many times do I have to tell you, it's not my fault! I just found out!"

THERESE:
Here, Mme. Dubuc, hide these!

ROSE:
How are things at your place, Ginette?

GINETTE:
Oh, same as usual, they fight all day long . . . Nothing

new. My mother still drinks . . . And my father gets
mad . . . And they go on fighting . . .

ROSE:

Poor kid . . . And your sister?

GINETTE:

Suzanne? Oh, she's still the brainy one. She can't do
anything wrong, you know? "Now there's a girl who uses
her head. You should be more like her, Ginette. She's
making something of her life" . . . Nobody else even
counts, especially me. But they always did like her best.
And, of course, now she's a teacher, you'd think she was
a saint or something.

ROSE:

Hey, come on, Ginette. Isn't that a bit much?

GINETTE:

No, I'm serious . . . My mother's never cared about me.
It's always, "Suzanne's the prettiest. Suzanne's the
nicest," . . . Day in, day out till I'm sick of it! Even Lise
doesn't like me anymore!

LINDA: *on the phone*

"Oh, go to hell! If you're not gonna listen, why should I
talk? Call me back when you're in a better mood!"

She hangs up.

For Chrissake, Aunt Rose, why didn't you tell me I was
wanted on the phone? Now he's pissed off at me!

ROSE:

Isn't she polite! You see how polite she is?

Spotlight on PIERRETTE.

PIERRETTE:

When I left home, I was head over heels in love, I couldn't even see straight. No one existed for me but Johnny. He made me waste ten years of my life, the bastard. I'm only thirty now and I feel like sixty. The things that guy got me to do! And me, the idiot, I listened to him. Did I ever. Ten years I worked his club for him. I was a looker, I brought in the customers, and that was fine as long as it lasted . . . But now . . . now I'm fucked. I feel like jumping off a bridge. All I got left is the bottle. And that's what I've been doing since Friday. Poor Lise, she thinks she's done for just 'cause she's pregnant. She's young, I'll give her my doctor's name . . . He'll fix her up. It'll be easy for her to start over. But not me. Not me. I'm too old. A girl who's been at it for ten years is washed up. Finished. And try telling that to my sisters. They'll never understand. I don't know what I'm gonna do now. I don't know.

LISE:

I don't know what I'm gonna do now. I don't know. An abortion, that's serious. I've heard enough stories to know that. But I guess I'm better off going to see Pierrette's doctor than trying to do it myself. Ah, why do these things always happen to me? Pierrette, she's lucky. Working in the same club for ten years, making a bundle . . . And she's in love! I wouldn't mind being in her shoes. Even if her family can't stand her, at least she's happy on her own.

PIERRETTE:

He dumped me, just like that! "It's finished", he said. "I don't need you anymore. You're too old and too ugly. So pack your bags and beat it". That son-of-a-bitch! He didn't leave me a nickel! Not a goddamn nickel! After all I did for him. Ten years! Ten years for nothing. That's enough to make anyone pack it in. What am I gonna do now, eh? What? Become a waitress at Kresge's like Lise? No thanks! Kresge's is fine for kids and old ladies, but not for me. I don't know what I'm gonna do. I just don't know. And here I've gotta pretend everything's great. But I can't tell Linda and Lise I'm washed up. *Silence.* Yeah . . . I guess there's nothing left but booze . . . good thing I like that . . .

LISE: *interspersed throughout PIERRETTE's last speech*
I'm scared, dear God, I'm scared!

She approaches PIERRETTE.

Are you sure this'll work, Pierrette? If you only knew how scared I am!

PIERRETTE: *laughing*
'Course it will. It'll be fine, kid. You'll see . . .

The lights come back up.

MARIE-ANGE:
It's not even safe to go to the show anymore. I went to the Rex the other day to see Belmondo in something, I forget what. I went alone, cause my husband didn't wanna go. Well, all of a sudden, right in the middle of the show this smelly old bum sits down next to me and starts grabbing my knee. You can imagine how embarrassed I was but that didn't stop me. I stood up, took my purse and smashed him right in his ugly face.

DES-NEIGES:
Good for you, Mme. Brouillette! I always carry a hat pin when I go to the show. You never know what'll happen. And the first one who tries to get fresh with me . . . But I've never used it yet.

ROSE:

Hey, Germaine, these Cokes are pretty warm.

GERMAINE:

When are you gonna stop criticizing, eh? When?

LISE:

Linda, you got a pencil and paper?

LINDA:

I'm telling you, Lise, don't do it!

LISE:

I know what I'm doing. I've made up my mind and nothing's gonna make me change it.

RHEAUNA: *to THERESE*

What are you doing there?

THERESE:

Shh! Not so loud! You should take some, too. Two or three books, she'll never know.

RHEAUNA:

I'm not a thief!

THERESE:

Come on, Mlle. Bibeau, it's not a question of stealing. She got these stamps for nothing and there's a million of 'em. A million!

RHEAUNA:

Say what you will, she invited us here to paste her stamps and we've got no right to steal them!

GERMAINE: *to ROSE*

What are those two talking about? I don't like all this whispering . . .

She goes over to RHEAUNA and THERESE.

THERESE: *seeing her coming*
Oh . . . Yeah . . . You add two cups of water and stir.

RHEAUNA:
What? *Noticing GERMAINE.* Oh! Yes! She was giving me a recipe.

GERMAINE:
A recipe for what?

RHEAUNA:
Doughnuts!

THERESE:
Chocolate pudding!

GERMAINE:
Well, which is it? Doughnuts or chocolate pudding?

She comes back to ROSE.

Listen, Rose, there's something fishy going on around here.

ROSE: *who has just hidden a few books in her purse*
Don't be silly . . . You're imagining things . . . .

GERMAINE:
And I think Linda's spending too much time with Pierrette. Linda, get over here!

LINDA:
In a minute, Ma . . . .

GERMAINE:
I said come here! That means now. Not tomorrow!

LINDA:

Okay! Don't get in a flap . . . so, what do you want?

GABRIELLE:

Stay with us a bit . . . You've been with your Aunt long enough.

LINDA:

So what?

GERMAINE:

What's going on between her and Lise there?

LINDA:

Oh . . . Nothing . . .

GERMAINE:

Answer when you're spoken to!

ROSE:

Lise wrote something down a while ago.

LINDA:

It was just an address . . .

GERMAINE:

Not Pierrette's, I hope! If I ever find out you've been to her place, you're gonna hear from me, got that?

LINDA:

Will you lay off! I'm old enough to know what I'm doing!

She goes back to PIERRETTE.

ROSE:

Maybe it's none of my business, Germaine, but . . .

GERMAINE:
Why, what's the matter now?

ROSE:
Your Linda's picking up some pretty bad habits . . .

GERMAINE:
You can say that again! But don't worry, Rose, I can handle her. She's gonna straighten out fast. And as for Pierrette, it's the last time she'll set foot in this house. I'll throw her down the goddamn stairs!

MARIE-ANGE:
Have you noticed Mme. Bergeron's daughter lately? Wouldn't you say she's been putting on weight?

LISETTE:
Yes, I've noticed that . . .

THERESE: *insinuating*
Strange, isn't it? It's all in her middle.

ROSE:
I guess the sap's running a bit early this year.

MARIE-ANGE:
She tries to hide it too. It's beginning to show, though.

THERESE:
And how! I wonder who could have done it?

LISETTE:
It's probably her step-father . . .

GERMAINE:
Wouldn't surprise me in the least. He's been after her ever since he married her mother.

THERESE:

It must be awful in that house. I feel sorry for Monique. She's so young . . .

ROSE:

Maybe so, but you must admit, she's been looking for it, too. Look how she dresses. Last summer, I was embarrassed to look at her! And you know me, I'm no prude. Remember those red shorts she had on, those short shorts? Well, I said it then, and I'll say it again, "Monique Bergeron is gonna turn out bad." She's got the devil in her, that girl, a real demon. Besides, she's a redhead . . . No, you can say what you like, those unwed mothers deserve what they get and I got no sympathy for 'em.

LISE starts to get up.

PIERRETTE:

Take it easy, kid!

ROSE:

It's true! It's their own damn fault! I'm not talking about the ones who get raped. That's different. But an ordinary girl who gets herself knocked up, uh! uh! . . . She gets no sympathy from me. It's too goddamn bad! I tell you, if my Carmen ever came home like that, she'd go sailing right through the window! Not that I'm worried about her, mind you. She's not that kind of girl . . . Nope, for me unwed mothers are all the same. A bunch of depraved sluts. You know what my husband calls 'em, eh? Cockteasers!

LISE:

I'll kill her if she doesn't shut up!

GINETTE:

Why? If you ask me, she's right.

LISE:
You shut your trap and get out of here!

PIERRETTE:
Isn't that a bit much, Rose?

ROSE:
Listen, Pierrette, we know you're an expert on these
matters. We know you can't be shocked. Maybe you
think it's normal, but we don't. There's one way to
prevent it . . .

PIERRETTE: *laughing*
There's lots of ways. Ever heard of the pill?

ROSE:
It's no use talking to you! That's not what I meant! I'm
against free love! I'm a Catholic! So leave us alone and
stay where you belong, filthy whore!

LISETTE:
I think perhaps you exaggerate, Mme. Ouimet. There are
occasions when girls can get themselves in trouble and
it's not entirely their fault.

ROSE:
You! You believe everything they tell you in those stupid
French movies!

LISETTE:
What have you got against French movies?

ROSE:
Nothing. I like English ones better, that's all. French
movies, they're too realistic, too far-fetched. You
shouldn't believe what they say. They always make you
feel sorry for the girl who gets pregnant. It's never

anyone else's fault. Well, do you feel sorry for tramps like that? I don't! A movie's a movie and life's life!

LISE:

I'll kill her, the bitch! Stupid fucking jerk! She goes around judging everyone and she's got the brains of a . . . And as for her Carmen. Well, I happen to know her Carmen and believe me, she does a lot more than tease! She oughtta clean her own house before she shits on everyone else.

Spotlight on ROSE OUIMET.

ROSE:

That's right. Life is life and no goddamn Frenchman ever made a movie about that! Sure, any old actress can make you feel sorry for her in a movie. Easy as pie! And when she's finished work, she can go home to her big fat mansion and climb into her big fat bed that's twice the size of my bedroom, for Chrissake! But the rest of us, when we get up in the morning . . . when I wake up in the morning he's lying there staring at me . . . Waiting. Every morning, I open my eyes and there he is, waiting! Every night, I get into bed and there he is, waiting! He's always there, always after me, always hanging over me like a vulture. Goddamn sex! It's never that way in the movies, is it? Oh no, in the movies it's always fun! Besides, who cares about a woman who's gotta spend her life with a pig just 'cause she said yes to him once? Well, I'm telling you, no fucking movie was ever this sad. Because movies don't last a lifetime! *Silence.* Why did I ever do it? Why? I should have said no. I should have yelled no at the top of my lungs and stayed an old maid. At least I'd have had some peace. I was so ignorant in those days. Christ, I didn't know what I was in for. All I could think of was "the Holy State of Matrimony!" You gotta be stupid to bring up your kids like that, knowing nothing. My Carmen won't get caught like that. Because I've been telling her for years what men are really worth. She won't be able to say I didn't warn her! *On the verge of tears.* She won't end up like me, forty-four years old, with a two year old kid and another one on the way, with a stupid slob of a husband who can't understand a thing, who demands his "rights" at least twice a day, three hundred and sixty-five days a year. When you get to be forty and you realize you've got nothing behind you and nothing ahead of you, it makes you want to dump everything and start all over . . . But women . . . women can't do that . . . They get grabbed by the throat, and they stay that way, right to the end!

The lights come back up.

GABRIELLE:
Well, I like French movies. They sure know how to make 'em good and sad. They make me cry every time. And you must admit, Frenchmen are a lot better looking than Canadians. They're real men!

GERMAINE:
Now wait just a minute! That's not true.

MARIE-ANGE:
Come on! The little peckers don't even come up to my shoulder. And they act like girls! Of course, what do you expect? They're all queer!

GABRIELLE:
I beg your pardon. Some of them are men! And I don't mean like our husbands.

MARIE-ANGE:
After hour husbands anything looks good.

LISETTE:
You don't mix serviettes with paper napkins.

GERMAINE:
Okay, so our husbands are rough, but our actors are just as good and just as good-looking as any one of those French fairies from France.

GABRIELLE:
Well, I wouldn't say no to Jean Marais. Now there's a real man!

OLIVINE:
Coke . . . Coke . . . More . . . Coke . . .

ROSE:
Hey, can't you shut her up? It's impossible to work! Shove a Coke in her mouth, Germaine. That'll keep her quiet.

GERMAINE:
I think I've run out.

ROSE:
Jesus, you didn't buy much, did you? Talk about cheap!

RHEAUNA: *as she steals some stamps*
Oh, what the heck. Three more books and I can get my chrome dustpan.

ANGELINE comes in.

ANGELINE:
Hello . . . *to RHEAUNA* I've come back . . .

THE OTHERS: *coldly*
Hello . . .

ANGELINE:
I went to see Father Castelneau . . .

PIERRETTE:
She didn't even look at me!

MARIE-ANGE:
What does she want with Mlle. Bibeau?

DES-NEIGES:
I'm sure it's to ask forgiveness. After all, Mlle. Sauvé is
a good person and she knows what's right. It'll all work
out for the best, you'll see.

GERMAINE:
While we're waiting, I'm gonna see how many books
we've filled.

The women sit up in their chairs. GABRIELLE
hesitates, then speaks.

GABRIELLE:
Oh, Germaine, I forgot to tell you. I found a corsetmaker.
Her name's Angélina Giroux. Come over here, I'll tell
you about her.

RHEAUNA:
I knew you'd come back to me, Angéline. I'm very
happy. You'll see, we'll pray together and the Good Lord
will forget all about it. God's not stupid, you know.

LISE:
That's it, Pierrette, they've made up.

PIERRETTE:
I'll be goddamned!

ANGELINE:

I'll just say goodbye to Pierrette and explain . . .

RHEAUNA:

No, you'd best not say another word to her. Stay with me and leave her alone. That chapter's closed.

ANGELINE:

Whatever you say.

PIERRETTE:

Well, that's that. She's won. Makes me want to puke. Nothing left for me to do here. I'm getting out of here.

GERMAINE:

Gaby, you're terrific. I'd almost given up hope. It's not everyone can make me a corset. I'll go see her next week.

She goes over to the box that is supposed to hold the completed books. The women follow her with their eyes.

My God, there isn't much here! Where are all the booklets? There's no more than a dozen in the box. Maybe they're . . . No, the table's empty!

Silence. GERMAINE looks at all the women.

What's going on here?

THE OTHERS:
Well . . . Ah . . . I don't know . . . Really . . .

They pretend to search for the books. GERMAINE stations herself in front of the door.

GERMAINE:
Where are my stamps?

ROSE:
I don't know, Germaine. Let's look for them.

GERMAINE:
They're not in the box and they're not on the table. I want to know what's happened to my stamps!

OLIVINE: *pulling stamps out from under her clothes*
Stamps? Stamps . . . . Stamps . . .

She laughs.

THERESE:
Mme. Dubuc, hide that . . . Goddamn it, Mme. Dubuc!

MARIE-ANGE:
Holy Ste.-Anne!

DES-NEIGES:
Pray for us!

GERMAINE:
But her clothes are full of them! What the . . . She's got them everywhere! Here . . . And here . . . . Thérèse . . . Don't tell me it's you.

THERESE:
Heavens, no! I swear, I had no idea!

GERMAINE:
Let me see your purse.

THERESE:
Really, Germaine, if that's all the faith you have in me.

ROSE:
Germaine, don't be ridiculous!

GERMAINE:
You too, Rose. I want to see your purse. I want to see all your purses. Every one of them!

DES-NEIGES:
I refuse! I've never been so insulted!

YVETTE:
Me neither.

LISETTE:
I'll never set foot in here again!

GERMAINE grabs THERESE's bag and opens it. She pulls out several books.

GERMAINE:
Ahah! I knew it! I bet it's the same with all of you! You bastards! You won't get out of here alive! I'll knock you to kingdom come!

PIERRETTE:
I'll help you, Germaine. Nothing but a pack of thieves! And they look down their noses at me!

GERMAINE:
Show me your purses.

She grabs ROSE's purse.

Look at that . . . And that!

She grabs another purse.

More here. And look, still more! You too, Mlle. Bibeau? There's only three, but even so!

ANGELINE:
Oh, Rhéauna, you too!

GERMAINE:
All of you, thieves! The whole bunch of you, you hear me? Thieves!

MARIE-ANGE:
You don't deserve all those stamps.

DES-NEIGES:
Why you more than anyone else?

ROSE:
You've made us feel like shit with your million stamps!

GERMAINE:
But those stamps are mine!

LISETTE:
They ought to be for everyone!

THE OTHERS:
Yeah, everyone!

GERMAINE:
But they're mine! Give them back to me!

THE OTHERS:
No way!

MARIE-ANGE:
There's lots more in the boxes. Let's help ourselves.

DES-NEIGES:
Good idea.

YVETTE:
I'm filling my purse.

GERMAINE:
Stop! Keep your hands off!

THERESE:
Here, Mme. Dubuc, take these! Here's some more.

MARIE-ANGE:
Come on, Mlle. Verrette. There's tons of them. Here.
Give me a hand.

PIERRETTE:
Let go of that!

GERMAINE:
My stamps! My stamps!

ROSE:
Help me, Gaby, I've got too many!

GERMAINE:
My stamps! My stamps!

> *A huge battle ensues. The women steal all the stamps
> they can. PIERRETTE and GERMAINE try to stop
> them. LINDA and LISE stay seated in the corner and
> watch without moving. Screams are heard as some of the
> women begin fighting.*

MARIE-ANGE:
Give me those, they're mine!

ROSE:
That's a lie, they're mine!

LISETTE: *to GABRIELLE*
Will you let go of me! Let me go!

They start throwing stamps and books at one another. Everybody grabs all they can get their hands on, throwing stamps everywhere, out the door, even out the window. OLIVINE DUBUC starts cruising around in her wheelchair singing "O Canada". A few women go out with their loot of stamps. ROSE and GABRIELLE stay a bit longer than the others.

GERMAINE:
My sisters! My own sisters!

GABRIELLE and ROSE go out. The only ones left in the kitchen are GERMAINE, LINDA and PIERRETTE. GERMAINE collapses into a chair.

My stamps! My stamps!

PIERRETTE puts her arms around GERMAINE's shoulders.

PIERRETTE:
Don't cry, Germaine.

GERMAINE:
Don't talk to me. Get out! You're no better than the rest of them!

PIERRETTE:
But . . .

GERMAINE:

Get out! I never want to see you again!

PIERRETTE:

But I tried to help you! I'm on your side, Germaine!

GERMAINE:

Get out and leave me alone! Don't speak to me. I don't
want to see anyone!

*PIERRETTE goes out slowly. LINDA also heads
towards the door.*

LINDA:

It'll be some job cleaning all that up!

GERMAINE:

My God! My God! My stamps! There's nothing left!
Nothing! Nothing! My beautiful new home! My lovely
furniture! Gone! My stamps! My stamps!

*She falls to her knees beside the chair, picking up the
remaining stamps. She is crying very hard. We hear all
the others outside singing "O Canada". As the song
continues, GERMAINE regains her courage. She
finishes "O Canada" with the others, standing at
attention, with tears in her eyes. A rain of stamps falls
slowly from the ceiling . . .*